Praise for Kit Pearson

"Kit Pearson is a great talent in Canadian children's literature."

—*The Guardian* (Charlottetown)

"One of Canada's best junior fiction writers."
—*The StarPhoenix* (Saskatoon)

"Pearson is a strong writer whose work puts to shame most of the books that kids spend so much time reading these days."

—*Ottawa Citizen*

"Kit Pearson gives young readers a strong testament of the interlocking nature and power of reading, writing and living."

—*The Vancouver Sun*

"Another magical tale from the master."

—*Toronto Star*

"Dazzle. It's not the right word for what Kit Pearson manages to do ... but it's close. Closer would be a word that catches the irregular glint of light reflected on water, street lights suspended in fog, an opalescent fracturing of time and genre to create something with its own unique glow."

—*Edmonton Journal*

PUFFIN CANADA

LOOKING AT THE MOON

KIT PEARSON was born in Edmonton and grew up there and in Vancouver. Her previous seven novels (six of which have been published by Penguin) have been published in Canada, in English and French, and in the United States, Australia, New Zealand, Japan, the Netherlands, Germany, Great Britain, China, and Korea. She has received fourteen awards for her writing, including the Vicky Metcalf Award for her body of work. She presently lives in Victoria.

Visit her website: www.kitpearson.com.

Also by Kit Pearson

The Daring Game

A Handful of Time

The Sky Is Falling

The Lights Go On Again

Awake and Dreaming

*This Land: An Anthology of Canadian Stories
for Young Readers*
(as editor)

*Whispers of War:
The War of 1812 Diary of Susanna Merritt*

A Perfect Gentle Knight

Looking at
the Moon

GUESTS OF WAR
BOOK TWO

KIT PEARSON

PUFFIN
CANADA

PUFFIN CANADA

Published by the Penguin Group

Penguin Group (Canada), 90 Eglinton Avenue East, Suite 700, Toronto, Ontario, Canada M4P 2Y3
(a division of Pearson Canada Inc.)

Penguin Group (USA) Inc., 375 Hudson Street, New York, New York 10014, U.S.A.
Penguin Books Ltd, 80 Strand, London WC2R 0RL, England
Penguin Ireland, 25 St Stephen's Green, Dublin 2, Ireland (a division of Penguin Books Ltd)
Penguin Group (Australia), 250 Camberwell Road, Camberwell, Victoria 3124, Australia
(a division of Pearson Australia Group Pty Ltd)
Penguin Books India Pvt Ltd, 11 Community Centre, Panchsheel Park, New Delhi – 110 017, India
Penguin Group (NZ), 67 Apollo Drive, Rosedale, North Shore 0632, Auckland, New Zealand
(a division of Pearson New Zealand Ltd)
Penguin Books (South Africa) (Pty) Ltd, 24 Sturdee Avenue, Rosebank, Johannesburg 2196,
South Africa

Penguin Books Ltd, Registered Offices: 80 Strand, London WC2R 0RL, England

First published in a Viking Canada hardcover by Penguin Group (Canada),
a division of Pearson Canada Inc., 1991
Published in Puffin Canada paperback by Penguin Group (Canada),
a division of Pearson Canada Inc., 1993
Published in this edition, 2007

1 2 3 4 5 6 7 8 9 10 (OPM)

Copyright © Kathleen Pearson, 1991

*Publisher's note: This book is a work of fiction. Names, characters, places and incidents
either are the product of the author's imagination or are used fictitiously, and any
resemblance to actual persons living or dead, events, or locales is entirely coincidental.*

Manufactured in the U.S.A.

ISBN-13: 978-0-14-305635-5
ISBN-10: 0-14-305635-2

Library and Archives Canada Cataloguing in Publication data available upon request.

Visit the Penguin Group (Canada) website at **www.penguin.ca**

Special and corporate bulk purchase rates available; please see
www.penguin.ca/corporatesales or call 1-800-810-3104, ext. 477 or 474

For Betty Anne and Ron

Sorting Out the Drummonds

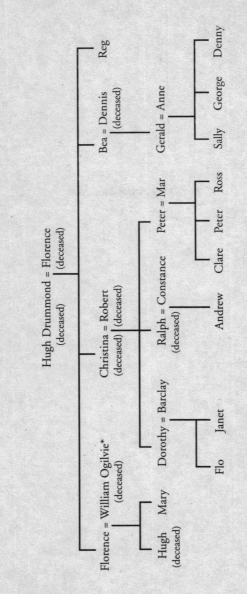

*Brother of "Aunt Catherine"

I whispered, "I am too young,"
And then, "I am old enough";
Wherefore I threw a penny
To find out if I might love.

O love is the crooked thing,
There is nobody wise enough
To find out all that is in it,
For he would be thinking of love
Till the stars had run away
And the shadows eaten the moon.
Ah, penny, brown penny, brown penny,
One cannot begin it too soon.

W.B. YEATS

Return to Gairloch

I look so ugly!

Norah peered over her brother's head at the photograph, while Aunt Mary held open the Toronto newspaper and read aloud from the "Personal Notes" for August 2, 1943:

> Mrs. Wm. Ogilvie, her daughter Miss Mary Ogilvie, and their young war guests, Norah and Gavin Stoakes, have just returned from a trip to Vancouver. They will be spending the month of August at "Gairloch," their summer home in Muskoka.

In the picture above the caption Aunt Florence sat stiffly on the chesterfield, looking as majestic as usual. Gavin was perched on its right arm and Aunt Mary smiled timidly on the far left. Between the two women scowled Norah, her face all nose, and her arms and legs as skinny as toothpicks.

"What does 'Wim' mean?" asked Gavin.

Aunt Florence laughed. "William, pet. It's an abbreviation." She took the paper from her daughter to examine it more closely. "Must you always frown, Norah? At least your new dress looks presentable. We'll buy two copies so we can send one to your parents. Won't that be nice?"

Norah shrugged. She ran out of Ford's Bay Store, where they had picked up the newspaper while they waited for the launch. Standing on the dock, she hooded her eyes with both hands and gazed hungrily out at the lake.

At last they'd arrived! The hot, hundred-mile drive from Toronto had seemed endless. Norah had smouldered with frustration while they wasted a whole hour in Orillia, having lunch with friends of the family. During the meal she'd made so many hints about the time that Aunt Florence had marched her out to the car and made her wait there without dessert.

After Orillia Gavin had slept, but Norah had squirmed in the back seat, while Aunt Florence nattered to her daughter about their friends' connections. "Let's see now ... Alma Bartlett married Harry Stone ... wasn't he the brother of William Stone?" For all of July, during their trip to British Columbia, Norah had been subjected to the same boring gossip. *Who cares?* she wanted to scream.

But now she watched the dancing waves and sniffed in the balsamy smell that was always her first sensation of being back in Muskoka. A breeze lifted her sticky hair. She knelt on the dock and dipped her hands in the clear water. She splashed it into her face, then took a drink. All summer she had been waiting to feel and taste the lake again.

And in a very short while she would be at Gairloch itself! She hadn't been there since last October; now that there was gas rationing, and you couldn't buy new tires, they no longer came up in May. Norah still hadn't forgiven Aunt Florence for cheating her out of a whole month on the island. And a month spent almost entirely in Aunt Florence's company had been too much to bear.

Norah was used to her guardian after living with her for almost three years. After a rough beginning they had reached a sort of truce. But lately Aunt Florence's fussiness had driven her wild. Kind Aunt Mary understood that Norah was growing up, but Aunt Florence still treated her like a child.

"I'm thirteen!" she had protested, when Aunt Florence had brought home the "presentable" dress before their journey—impossibly babyish, with puffed sleeves and a sash. "I'm a teen-ager now—why can't I pick my *own* clothes?"

"A teen-ager!" Aunt Florence had sniffed. "I don't hold with these newfangled notions. There's no such thing as a teen-ager. In our family you are a child until you leave home and then you're an adult. I don't want to hear that word again."

And all Norah could respond was "Yes, Aunt Florence," as sulkily as she dared. Whenever she tried to explain *her* side of things, Aunt Florence just said "Sauce!" and closed the conversation. Norah remembered having loud, satisfying arguments with her mother. But her mother was in England and Norah hadn't seen her since she and Gavin had been sent to Canada to be safe from the war. With Aunt Florence she was supposed to behave like a polite guest and keep her mouth shut.

At last the launch curved around the headland, and Norah saw her "cousins" Janet and Flo in it, waving. She shouted and waved back and jumped away her car stiffness. Now she had five whole weeks of freedom ahead of her, when she could have as little as possible to do with bossy adults. She glanced down at the comfortable shorts she was only allowed to wear up north. Maybe she didn't *really* want to be a teen-ager, not yet …

"Norah, Norah!" Janet was leaning over the bow screaming her name. The spray flew into her mouth, making her choke. Flo pulled her back and waved.

All summer Aunt Florence had nagged at Norah to smile more often. Now she grinned so hugely her cheeks felt as if they were cracking. There had been "cousins" in Vancouver, but they were all boys and not very friendly. Flo and Janet were like real cousins. Sometimes Flo seemed distant—she was seventeen—but Janet was only a year older than Norah.

As soon as the launch putted up beside the dock, Janet leaped out and grabbed Norah, whirling her around. "Oh, *Norah,* you've finally come! It's been so boring without you!"

"Hi, kiddo," smiled Flo, tying up the boat efficiently. "Thank goodness you're here—now I can get this pesky sister out of my way."

"Your hair's longer!" cried Janet. "I like it. Do you like

mine? I put it in pincurls now." Janet's hair was a blonde
fuzz that emphasized her fat cheeks. She hugged Norah
again, then controlled her excitement as the aunts and
Gavin, loaded down with bags of groceries, came out of
the store.

"Hello Janet, hello Florence." The cousins were kissed
and exclaimed over. Gavin beamed up at everyone, his
eyes the same bright blue as the water.

"You might have helped us carry these, Norah," said
Aunt Florence. Norah ignored her as they all found places
in the long boat. She ran her hands over its mahogany
sides and leather seats. The launch was called *Florence*—
not after Aunt Florence but after her mother. But Norah
thought it suited her guardian to have the same name as
the luxurious boat, whose luminous wood, thick glass
windscreen and shiny brass all glittered with importance.

She watched carefully as Flo turned the key to start
the ignition. Only the older teen-agers were allowed to
drive the *Florence,* but you could run the smaller launch
by yourself when you turned thirteen. She hoped the
grown-ups would remember that before she had to
remind them.

"Isn't it great to be back?" whispered Gavin. He leaned
against Norah and the two of them threw their faces back
to drink in the spray, keeping watch for their first glimpse
of the island.

ALL OF THE DRUMMOND CLAN were on the dock to greet
them. Aunt Florence stepped out regally and accepted the

homage of her sisters, brother, in-laws, nieces and nephews as if she were their ruling monarch—which, being the eldest, she was. Norah barely noticed which of the crowd of grown-ups was kissing her. She was too busy taking in the white dock, the grey boathouse with its fancy railing and, best of all, the circular cottage waiting above.

"*Bosley!* Look, Norah, he remembers me! Wave, Boz!" Uncle Reg's black-and-white springer spaniel had bounded onto the dock and leapt at Gavin. Then he lifted one of his paws in greeting while everyone laughed.

Norah kicked off her shoes, wriggled through the excited group and ran up to the cottage. The stone steps were cool and rough under her tender feet. She dashed into the kitchen.

"Hanny! We're back!"

Hanny, Aunt Florence's cook in the city, turned around from the stove and opened her arms. Norah ran into them and their noses collided. They both laughed.

"Norah, what a treat to see you again! Did you have a grand trip? I got all your postcards, and Gavin's too—where is he?"

"Down at the dock, still being kissed," grinned Norah. She circled the spacious kitchen, grabbed a cookie off a plate and plopped herself on top of the old pine table, munching noisily.

"Not before dinner and no sitting on my clean table," said Hanny automatically, but her lined face still smiled. "Oh *my*, I've missed you all this month—even Mrs. O! The family seems rudderless without her here."

"How is Mr. Hancock?" asked Norah politely. Hanny's husband was retired, but he always came up with her in the summers to help out.

"Having a nice, lazy time as usual. He gads about fetching mail or taking your uncles fishing, while I slave away in a hot kitchen. Though I must say your aunts are very helpful." Hanny pushed her untidy hair under its net and turned back to the stove. "Now, Norah, it's lovely to see you but we'll have to talk later. You're all eating together this evening—all twenty of you!—and I'm not nearly ready. You'd better skedaddle—unless you'd like to peel some carrots."

Norah left quickly in case Hanny meant it. Before the family came in she made a swift inspection of the rest of the cottage: up the stairs and down the slippery hall, peeking into each of the huge bedrooms, then through the sunny dining room into the living room.

Nothing had changed; nothing ever did. Old photographs dotted the panelled walls. Cups from regattas, faded rugs and comfortable wicker furniture filled the dim space. A faint smell of wood smoke came from the massive stone fireplace. In an alcove beside it was the same wooden puzzle that had been there for years, its pieces scattered on a small table. Above it was Aunt Florence's mother's collection of china cats, and the knot board where all the children, including Norah, had learned to tie knots.

Norah ended her tour on the verandah, her favourite part of the cottage. She ran all around its wide circumference, then leaned against one of its thick cedar posts and watched the clan parade up the steps—as if she, not Aunt Florence, were the ruler of Gairloch.

Surely, the black cloud of angry misery that had hung over her almost constantly since she had turned thirteen would now dissolve.

2

The Cousins

*T*he long evening meal was over, the younger children had gone to bed, and the two generations of aunts and uncles, whom Flo had long ago christened "the Elders," were relaxing in the living room.

Norah sat on the rug opposite Janet, her calm mood already vanished. She was trying to concentrate on a game of slapjack, but inside she seethed at what Aunt Mar, her least favourite Elder, had just said to her in the kitchen.

"Look how you've grown, Norah! You'd better ask Aunt Florence to buy you a brassiere before school starts."

How dare she make personal remarks like that! At least the two of them had been alone, bringing out the dessert plates.

Norah tugged angrily at the skirt Aunt Florence had made her change into. The Elders changed for dinner every night, but the children only had to when they had what the younger cousins called a Big Dinner together.

It wasn't dark yet and Norah hadn't even had time to explore. She kept glancing out at the beckoning evening. Finally she couldn't bear to be inside a moment longer.

"I'm going for a walk," she whispered to Janet. She slipped out of the room and ran down to the boathouse to change. Comfortable again in slacks, an old shirt and bare feet, Norah strode along the shoreline path that circled the island. A chipmunk skittered out of her way and soft pine needles crunched under her feet.

Soon she reached the tiny log cabin that was the children's playhouse. No one seemed to have used it since she and Janet, with Bob and Alec—cousins on the Ogilvie side—had called themselves the Hornets and pretended the playhouse was a gangsters' hideaway. But this summer Bob and Alec hadn't come.

Four yellow-and-black striped masks hung on nails inside the door. Norah closed it quickly. It seemed much longer than a year ago that they had played that silly game.

Beyond the playhouse was the babies' beach. Norah rolled up her pant legs and paddled, her feet stirring up silt. The bay was so shallow that it looked brown, every ripple of sand showing through its crystal surface.

Her next stop was the gazebo perched on a rocky point at the far end of the island. An empty cup and saucer had been abandoned on the bench inside. Norah knew she should take them back to the kitchen, but that would slow her down.

She passed the windmill which pumped up water for the tank behind the cottage. Then she cut through the woods in the middle of the island, weaving through tree trunks and ferns until she reached a clearing. Here stood two extra cabins for overflowing family and guests. Behind them was Norah's favourite place on the island, the high rocky promontory that overlooked it all. Her feet reached for the familiar footholds as she scrabbled up the rock to the level platform on top. There she collapsed, panting and sweaty.

She ran her hands over the streaky pink rock and gazed down at the massed green foliage beneath her. Beyond it stretched the lake. Clumps of land—other islands and long fingers of mainland—broke up its flat expanse.

Vast as it was, this lake was the smallest of three huge ones that were joined together by narrow ribbons of water. But their lake was the deepest, Norah thought with satisfaction, and the most beautiful. She never tired of watching its colour change from silver to blue to green. Now its surface reflected the pink-tinged sky. The slanting light picked out each rock, tree and wave.

Norah let out a relieved breath—finally she was alone.

Her first encounter with the Drummond clan each summer was always overwhelming. Ten adults and eight children were here this month and they were all related. Norah had heard the expression "blood is thicker than water"; Ogilvie and Drummond blood seemed thicker than most. Over the summers she had grown used to the family's established rituals, jokes and conflicts. She knew as well as all the cousins that Aunt Bea was shrill and giddy because she resented Aunt Florence being the eldest, and that Uncle Reg played practical jokes on his two sisters whenever he had the chance.

But although the family was always warm towards their two war guests, Norah often felt as though they belonged to an exclusive club she and Gavin could never join. Every once in a while the family shared something that excluded them. This evening, for example, they had all started talking about Andrew, an unknown cousin who was supposed to arrive tomorrow. Andrew's funny expressions when he was four, the time he ran away and hid under the canoe when he was eight, the plays he made up ... all through dinner they had discussed him.

But Aunt Mar's rude comment had been much worse than the chatter about Andrew. Norah knew she needed a brassiere; she just couldn't bring herself to ask Aunt Florence for one. And anyway, shouldn't Aunt Florence notice for herself and suggest it?

It was difficult to believe that the two mounds on her chest, that had appeared almost overnight, really belonged to *her*. This last year she was sure her nose had grown as well. It seemed to fill up her whole face like a beak.

Dad had a nose like that—but it didn't matter on a man. Thinking of Mum and Dad produced the usual small ache, like prodding a sore spot. When she and Gavin finally went back to England, would her parents recognize this new person with a beaky nose and breasts like a woman's?

One day in the spring, as she was waiting nervously to attend her first mixed party, Norah had asked Aunt Florence if she was pretty. She knew Aunt Florence would tell her the truth; she didn't believe in false flattery.

"You are when you smile," was the brisk reply.

That meant she *wasn't* pretty, for if she always had to smile to enhance her looks, she couldn't be. It was also an infuriating way for Aunt Florence to get in some advice, instead of just answering the question.

Now she scraped away lichen from the rock. Why wasn't the magic of Gairloch making her troubles disappear, the way it usually did?

Tired of her own thoughts, Norah slithered back down the rock. She would go and check on Gavin. All of the boys except the two youngest ones slept in half of the old servants' quarters behind the cottage. The Hancocks slept in the other half. Norah poked her head into the large room that the family called the "Boys' Dorm." With Bob and Alec away, only three small boys, Peter, Ross and Gavin, occupied cots. All three were fast asleep.

Norah went in and bent over Gavin. As usual he clutched "Creature," his toy elephant, in his fist. She covered him up more closely. Even though the gentle little boy was everyone's favourite, the family accepted that Norah was the one who was really responsible for him. She had never forgotten how she had neglected that responsibility when she'd first come to Canada. Now her love for Gavin was the most constant element in her life here.

She heard laughter coming from the water's edge; the others must have already gone to bed. Norah wished she could go straight down to the boathouse, where all the girls slept, but one of the family rituals was saying good-night.

Aunt Anne and Uncle Gerald, who stayed in one of the cabins with their two youngest children, had already retired. The rest of the Elders were playing bridge.

"I'm going to bed now," Norah announced.

"I was just going to call you," said Aunt Florence. "What were you doing out there all by yourself? Janet was upset you left so abruptly."

Norah shrugged. On the first night back at Gairloch you were expected to kiss everyone. Dutifully she made her rounds. "Good-night Aunt Florence ... Aunt Mary ... Aunt Catherine ... Aunt Bea ... Aunt Dorothy ... Uncle Barclay ... Uncle Reg ... Aunt Mar." Whew! Eight kisses, some on papery cheeks or rough skin that needed a shave.

She fled to the toilet, then down to the dock. The boathouse was built directly over the lake. On this side of the island the water was so deep that the boats could be driven right into their slips, like putting a car in the garage. Before she went up the stairs, Norah paused to admire the family's fleet. Inside, the *Florence* bobbed beside the smaller launch—the *Putt-Putt*—and the heavy old rowboat. The sailboat was moored outside and the canoe was overturned against a wall.

She looked for her mug and toothbrush on the shelf built under the window. It was in the same place it had been last Thanksgiving. Norah brushed her teeth vigorously and cleaned the brush in the lake. Ignoring the bar of soap beside the mug, she splashed her face and dried herself with the fresh towel waiting for her on her hook.

She stood for a moment, listening to the haunting wail of a loon. A few stars had already appeared and the fat moon made a silver trail on the water. Norah drank in a gulp of cool night air, then climbed up the stairs to the "Girls' Dorm."

The familiar space seemed to welcome her. Everything was the same: the messy clutter of clothes and bathing suits, the dark wooden walls, the nails to hang their things on and the faded gingham curtains they always left open.

"Where have *you* been?" Clare asked her. "Moongazing? Maybe our Norah has been having romantic thoughts."

Norah pulled off her clothes and got into her pyjamas without answering. Clare was so impossible, no one took her seriously. She was sitting on the edge of her bed, plucking at her ukelele and yowling "You Are My Sunshine" out of tune.

"*Please* stop, Clare," begged Sally. "I'm trying to go to sleep."

Clare's pretty, pouty face looked up. "Then go back to the cabin with your parents and little brothers," she said rudely. "If you want to be out here with the *big* girls, you have to put up with us." She began again, even louder.

Abashed, Sally sank down into her pillow. She was only seven and in awe of her older cousins. But Flo reached over and snatched away Clare's ukelele.

"You're too noisy," she said calmly. Ignoring Clare's protests, she blew out the lamp. "Get into bed, everyone, and keep quiet so Sally can go to sleep."

The five girls lay in bed for a few silent moments. The loon warbled again and something, a frog or a fish, splashed briefly. Waves lapped soothingly against the sides of the boathouse. Norah snuggled farther into her narrow but cosy bed, feeling as usual as if she were *on* a boat. She began to think of the treats that waited for her tomorrow … the first of a long string of days when there was nothing she *had* to do.

Then, as usual, they all began talking again, as revived and wide-awake as if they had had hours of sleep. Only Sally dozed. The others sat up in bed, their faces white ovals in the moonlight.

First Flo, Janet and Clare finished telling Norah everything she had missed in July: the Port Clarkson Regatta, the *Ahmic* steamship accident, and how Uncle Gerald had seen a bear swimming from one island to another.

"Aunt Bea tried to organize us like Aunt Florence," giggled Janet.

"We had to recite *poetry* every night," complained Clare. "It was terrible."

"I hate to admit it, but it's a relief to have Aunt Florence back," said Flo. "Now it's your turn, Norah. Tell us all about your trip!"

Norah began with the only good part—the train. They had slept in narrow bunks with straps to hold them in; the train rocked them to sleep every night like a noisy cradle. "The meals were *wonderful,* and really fancy, just like in a restaurant. There were white tablecloths and finger bowls and we had roast beef and trout and things like that."

She couldn't find words to describe her astonishment at how huge Canada was; the train seemed to go on forever, unfolding mile after mile of empty country. She remembered her first awestruck glimpse of the Rockies, their sharp peaks outlined against a hard blue sky.

Nor could she explain how being on the train had made her realize that, in a way that hadn't been true when she had first come to this country, the war seemed to have finally touched Canada. Every day she and Gavin walked the length of the whole train, through crowded cars full of soldiers and solitary, worried-looking women who soothed crying children.

She went on to describe Vancouver with its rounded mountains rising straight up from the sea; and the Ogilvie cousins whom the Drummonds had never met.

"Vancouver was sort of like England," said Norah. "But there was nothing to do there except visit a lot of boring relatives. Do you know they even had blackouts? After Pearl Harbor, because they're so close to Japan."

Clare interrupted her. "Did you know that I have a boy friend, Norah? Now that I'm fifteen, I'm finally allowed to date. His name's John and he's planning to join the RCAF. He's—"

"Spare us the details," Flo broke in. "We're already so tired of hearing about him."

"But *Norah* hasn't heard," persisted Clare. She continued to go on about how dreamy her new boy friend was until Flo interrupted her again.

"You don't even know what loving someone is," she said quietly. "Wait until he *does* join up. Like Ned ..."

"Who's Ned?" Norah asked, because she knew Flo wanted her to.

"He's *my* boy friend, and he's in the army and stationed overseas. I write to him three times a week."

"She also writes to two other boys," said Janet. "She uses so much paper that Mother makes her buy her own."

"Well, it's important," said Flo. "They need to be cheered up."

Norah turned over impatiently. Flo seemed much more grown-up this summer, as if she had already entered the strange adult world that was still closed to the rest of them. And she wished all of them would stop going on about *boys*. They were just like her friend Dulcie. This past year Dulcie had "discovered" boys. She was always moaning about being too young to go to dances, and she didn't understand when Norah said she wasn't interested. At least Janet wasn't like that yet.

But then Janet disappointed her too.

"What do you think of Frankie, Norah?" she asked. "I think he's the greatest thing since canned peas."

Flo roared with laughter. "Sorry, Janet," she choked, seeing her sister's hurt face. "But when you try to use expressions like that you sound so—"

"I don't want to hear how I sound," interrupted Janet huffily. "I was asking Norah a question. What do you think of Frankie?"

Norah knew she meant Frank Sinatra. "He's okay, I guess," she sighed. She didn't mind the mellow voice which seemed to be on the radio every time it was turned on. But she was tired of him. Her other city friend, Paige, had every one of his records and played them until Norah wanted to scream. At least they didn't have a phonograph in the boathouse.

The conversation turned to a comparison of their school years in Montreal and Toronto. They had a lot to catch up on since last summer.

"Stop *talking*," moaned Sally, turning over and going back to sleep. Norah herself was drifting through whole patches of conversation. Then Janet asked her a question. "Have you ever met Andrew, Norah? I can't remember if you were here the last time he came."

"No, I haven't. Who *is* this Andrew, anyway?" she added irritably.

"He's the only son of Uncle Ralph and Aunt Constance," explained Flo. "Uncle Ralph was my mother's and Clare's father's brother—he died about five years ago. They used to come to Gairloch every summer but then Aunt Constance married again and Andrew had to move to Winnipeg. He's been back a few times for a visit. And tomorrow he'll be here again! He's transferring to the University of Toronto this fall."

"He's *dreamy*," said Clare. "He visited us in Montreal last year and all my friends were envious. If he wasn't my cousin I'd have a huge crush on him."

"He's the best person in the family," said Flo. "We were really close when we were kids."

"The last time he came he taught me how to dive," said Janet. "Wait till you see how handsome he is, Norah!"

Norah pretended she was already asleep. What a bore this Andrew sounded! And what a bore the cousins were going to be, if all they wanted to talk about were boys and singers.

And yet, since she was now a teen-ager too, shouldn't she be more interested in those things? She didn't want to be as childish as Sally or as grown-up as Flo. But it wasn't much fun to flounder in between.

3

A Strange Story

The jubilant clamour of birds, much louder than in the city, woke Norah early. She peeked out of the window at the fresh morning and decided to go for her first swim of the summer.

A few minutes later she was balancing on the edge of the diving board, fastening the strap of her bathing cap and admiring how the ripples broke up the sunlight into a sparkling web. Then she bounced up and down, pointed her arms straight up and plummeted into the lake.

She struggled up through the icy depths and spat out air and water. For a few minutes she thrust vigorously away from land. Once she was used to the temperature, she swam back slowly, staring at the way her limbs looked green below the surface of the water. She ducked her head under and twisted and somersaulted like an otter. Swimming at an indoor pool in the winter could never match this.

Seizing her towel, Norah scrubbed warmth back into her tingling skin. This afternoon the water would be warmer; she wondered if she could still make it to Little

Island and back. When she'd first come to Canada, she'd barely been able to swim. The sea at Grandad's, where she'd spent almost every summer in England, had been too rough to do much but paddle. But now she was as good as Bob and Alec. She sighed, missing them. She wouldn't be able to have races with Janet and Clare, who were both good swimmers but lazy.

"I bet it was cold," yawned Flo, as Norah rushed back into the Girls' Dorm to change.

Norah grinned as she tugged off her bathing suit and flung on her clothes. "Not for me! Maybe for sissy Canadians ..." Everyone leapt out of bed and began a pillow fight. This was more like old times: larking around, not mooning about boys.

When the breakfast gong sounded, Norah left the others to get dressed. She sped up the hill to the cottage and was the first one to sit down at the children's table.

"Hungry, are you?" Hanny came out from the kitchen, set a bowl of oatmeal in front of Norah and sat down beside her with her cup of tea. "I've missed my good eater. The other girls are always on diets, except for Janet. And she should be!"

Norah began to tell Hanny about the trip to Vancouver. Their peaceful conversation was interrupted by Aunt Dorothy hurrying in. Meals at Gairloch were usually in shifts. The children ate first and the adults wandered in as they were finishing; all except Aunt Florence and old Aunt Catherine, who had breakfast in bed. Each of the other aunts took turns coming down early to help Hanny.

In a few minutes the long table was crowded with eight children. Sunlight streamed through the windows that spanned three walls of the dining room. Norah helped herself to a fourth piece of toast and spread it thickly with Hanny's "Muskoka Jam"—a delicious combination of wild blueberries and raspberries. Since food was rationed in Canada now, they had bacon once a week instead of every morning and were only allowed to put butter on one piece of toast. Norah preferred jam anyway; the butter tasted weird because Hanny stretched it with gelatin and evaporated milk.

She knew it was much worse in England. Her parents wrote that they ate tasteless grey government bread, only got a meagre amount of meat and butter each week, and never saw oranges or bananas. Even though the Ogilvies regularly sent food and clothing parcels to her family, Norah often felt guilty, knowing she was so much better fed and dressed.

Lately she'd been feeling guilty for another reason. It wasn't just the war that made her real family different. Her Canadian family was *wealthy*. Norah had never known, before she came here, anyone who had an enormous house in the city, one just as big for the holidays, and a boathouse that would hold her own house in England. Or a private telephone and a refrigerator and a car, and new, store-bought clothes as soon as you outgrew your old ones. Gavin had so many toys he regularly gave them away to "Bundles for Britain." Norah had a fancy bicycle, skates and a toboggan, a closet full of expensive dresses and a whole bookcase full of her own books.

Of course not everyone in Canada had this plenty. Her friend Bernard wore patched clothes and lived in a cramped apartment. And she'd heard people on the train to Vancouver complain about not having homes at all.

It wasn't right, that some people had too much and some not enough. The trouble was—and this always made Norah squirm—she *enjoyed* the luxuries she now had: the food, the books, her own room and above all, Gairloch.

Norah sighed and took another piece of toast. What was the point of feeling guilty for something that wasn't her fault? She hadn't wanted to come to Canada in the first place; but since she was here, she decided, she might as well appreciate all of this while she still had it.

"What time is Andrew coming?" Janet asked her mother.

"Late afternoon," said Aunt Dorothy. "Some of you can go in the launch when Mr. Hancock picks him up at the train."

"Is he going to sleep in the Boys' Dorm?" asked Peter. "There's lots of room."

"No, Peter, Andrew's too old to sleep with you. Florence said he could use the other cabin, since no one's there this month. And you little boys are not to disturb him. We want him to have a good rest before he starts classes."

Hanny brought Aunt Dorothy her tea. "I've made his favourite dessert for tonight. He was always fond of my snow pudding. It'll be just like the old days to have Andrew here again."

"Remember when he swam all the way around the island?" said Clare.

"He was the first person to do it since Hugh," said Flo proudly.

Norah glanced at Gavin, who was eating quietly. Once again the two of them were being left out. Everyone talked about this Andrew as if he were some kind of hero.

Aunt Anne and Uncle Gerald came into the cottage with the two youngest cousins, George and Denny.

"Mummy," said Sally immediately, as Aunt Anne tied on her brothers' bibs. "Can I sleep in the Boys' Dorm instead of the boathouse?"

Aunt Anne looked worried. "But why, Sally? You begged and begged to sleep with the girls instead of us, and you've only been out there for one night—don't you like it?"

"No," said Sally bluntly. "They're too noisy—especially Clare. They keep me awake and all they talk about is love. Why can't I sleep with Gavin and Peter and Ross?"

Gavin smiled at her; Sally was his best friend in the summers. "Please, can she, Aunt Anne?" he asked shyly. "*We* won't keep her awake, I promise."

"Well, perhaps it makes more sense to have all the younger ones together," said Aunt Anne. "But it's never been done before—the boys and girls have always slept separately. Why don't you just come back to the cabin, Sally?"

"No!" protested Sally. "You said I was old enough to sleep on my own! But I'd rather be with my *friends*."

"I suppose it would be all right," said her mother. "I'll have to ask Aunt Florence, then we'll see."

Norah sighed; all this fuss over a simple change in routine. Of course Sally should sleep with the younger cousins. It seemed so ridiculous to have to get Aunt Florence's approval, but Aunt Anne, the youngest and most timid in-law, had always been frightened of her.

Norah turned to Aunt Anne's husband, placidly eating his porridge. "Uncle Gerald, could you test me on the boat so I can use it by myself?"

"Glad to," he murmured through a mouthful. "Why don't you meet me on the dock in an hour?"

"Why, Norah, I'd forgotten you were thirteen!" Aunt Dorothy gazed at Norah, and at her daughters and Clare, with misty eyes. "You're all growing up much too fast."

More Elders began to fill the dining room. They all kissed their own children.

"How's my princess?" asked Uncle Barclay, leaning over Janet. She pulled on his moustache and giggled. Norah bent her head to hide her envy. In Canada she had plenty of mothers—almost too many—but no one could match the close relationship she'd had with her father.

Then Aunt Mary came in and kissed her and Gavin. This is the *kissiest* family, Norah thought impatiently.

"Norah, could you take up Miss Ogilvie's breakfast?" Hanny asked.

Glad to escape, she carefully ascended the stairs with the heavy tray. "Aunt Catherine," she said softly when she reached her door.

"Come in, dear," called a deep, hoarse voice. Aunt Catherine, the oldest person at Gairloch, was sitting up in bed with a book.

"It's Norah this morning—how pleasant! Sit down and talk to me while I eat."

Norah sat cross-legged on the bedspread, leaning against the white iron footboard. Tiny Aunt Catherine always looked so comical in bed. She wore round glasses and a pink nightcap, and her sharp eyes peered out from its flounces as if she were Red Riding Hood's grandmother.

Aunt Catherine was Norah's next favourite after Aunt Mary. She and Norah were both outsiders; the old woman was Aunt Florence's late husband's elder sister, so she wasn't related to the rest of the family. She had never married and Norah thought she'd had a much more interesting life than any of the other aunts. She had grown up in Glasgow and taught for years in a Scottish girls' school. After she'd retired she had travelled all over the world before she settled with her niece in Ottawa. She was the only grown-up Norah had ever met who confided in her as if there were no age difference between them.

Aunt Catherine still had traces of a British accent; that was another bond between them. Unlike Gavin, Norah had never completely lost her accent—she held onto it on purpose, determined not to lose that last link with home.

"Well, Norah, are you glad to be back?" the old woman asked.

"Oh, *yes*! I hated missing July!"

"I don't blame you. But I think it was a good idea of Florence's to show you and Gavin some of the rest of Canada. You don't want to go back to England only knowing Ontario. Did you read any good books while you were away?"

Aunt Catherine always asked *important* questions, not "Did you have a good time?" like all the others. Norah chatted to her about *The Three Musketeers*. Immersing herself in it last month had been the only way she could escape from Aunt Florence.

"I have a book here you might like," said Aunt Catherine. "I think you're old enough for it now. I loved it when I was your age, perhaps because the heroine's name is Catherine! It's called *Wuthering Heights*. Look in my bookcase—that green volume on the right."

Norah found *Wuthering Heights* and brought it back to the bed, examining it doubtfully. The print was small and the cover plain. She flipped through the pages and her eyes caught the words "Whatever our souls are made of, his and mine are the same ..."

"This isn't about love or anything like that, is it?" she asked suspiciously.

"Oh, Norah," laughed Aunt Catherine. "You are a one. It's *all* about love. Put it back and wait until next summer."

"I have a new Angela Brazil book to read, anyhow,"

said Norah. "Aunt Mary bought it for me. And there are lots of Agatha Christies in the living room."

"Then you'll be fine. Doesn't it make you feel *safe* to know you have enough to read? If I didn't always have a book waiting, I'd panic."

She put down her teacup and looked out the window. "What a perfect day for Andrew to arrive. Have you ever met him?"

Norah shook her head impatiently. Even Aunt Catherine was going to spoil her first day back with talk about this intruder.

Gavin appeared at the door. "Norah, Aunt Florence would like to see you." He must have already taken up her tray and had his usual morning visit with her.

Norah frowned. What could Aunt Florence want? It was almost time to meet Uncle Gerald at the dock. She left Gavin in her place, earnestly telling Aunt Catherine how Creature had nearly been left behind in Vancouver.

Aunt Florence's room was at the end of the long hall that had seven bedrooms off it. Norah knocked at her door.

"Come in, Norah." She was dressed perfectly and elegantly as usual, even though she was still in bed; her pink satin nightgown and matching dressing gown added to her queenly air. Every silver curl of her hair was in place.

Norah went over and pecked her cheek. Then she glanced meaningfully at the blue and green brightness beyond the window.

"Yes, I know you want to get outside, but it won't go away. Sit down, please, Norah. I promise I won't keep you long, but there's something I have to tell you."

Norah tried to control her sigh. She pulled over a chair—you never sat on Aunt Florence's bed—and waited. Then her heart lurched: had something happened at home?

"Is it—is it bad news?" she whispered.

"Oh *no,* Norah dear—I'm so sorry if I scared you!" Aunt Florence leaned over and patted her knee. "No bad news, nothing at all like that. This is something your mother wanted me to tell you and I'm afraid I've put it off. It's a matter that really only your mother *should* talk to you about. But she didn't want to do it in a letter, so she wrote and asked me to. I should have brought it up earlier but I keep forgetting how fast you're growing …"

Norah scuffed her feet. Uncle Gerald was probably waiting for her by now. What was her guardian going on about in such a roundabout way?

"What it is …" Aunt Florence looked hopeful. "Perhaps Flo and the others have already mentioned it, or you've read about it in one of the magazines you girls read."

Mentioned *what*? Norah never read the boring magazines that Clare always had around. She shook her head.

"Well, then, I'll have to explain. It's something that happens to you when you're around thirteen—although Mary didn't get it until she was fifteen. It happens to everyone every woman, that is—and we just have to put up with it." Aunt Florence took a deep breath and then her rich voice took on a storytelling quality. "Every girl and every woman has a little room inside of her. As the month goes by the little room gets untidy, and then a little visitor comes and sweeps it out clean. Then it becomes untidy again until the visitor comes again the next month. Now when *your* little visitor comes—and it might not even be this summer, but it will probably be this year— you *will* come and tell me so I can get you equipped, all right? I've brought all you need with me, just in case."

Norah just gaped at her. Then, because Aunt Florence seemed to expect an answer, she nodded.

"*That's* all right, then. I'll write to your mother and tell her I've prepared you. Run along now—you can take my tray with you."

Norah carried the tray down to the kitchen, then escaped outside. Aunt Florence was *nuts*! What on earth had she been talking about? Perhaps this was some weird Ogilvie or Drummond or Canadian fairy tale. Really, this family was very *odd* sometimes.

SHE FORGOT Aunt Florence's strange talk in her glee at being pronounced an expert boat-handler by Uncle Gerald. He went out with Norah in the *Putt-Putt* and made sure she knew how to start and stop the engine and how to fill it with gas. Then he reviewed the safety rules and watched as she drove the boat around Little Island all by herself.

"Well done!" he smiled. Norah asked permission to go out alone again and she spent a blissful half-hour driving to Ford's Bay and back. Whenever she passed another boat, she carefully took one hand off the steering wheel and waved.

Then she went out again with Janet and Bosley. The spaniel's ears streamed backwards as he perched happily on the bow. They landed on Little Island and explored every inch of it. Then they flopped down on the narrow shore, their heads resting on a mossy log and their feet in the water. Bosley leapt around them, chasing dragonflies.

"We should have brought a picnic," complained Janet. "I can't last much longer without something to eat. Norah ... do you think I'm fat?"

Norah turned her head and examined her friend. She couldn't say Janet *wasn't* fat—she was fatter than ever. But she didn't want to hurt her feelings.

"Well ..." she began.

"I'm fat," sighed Janet. "You're so lucky, Norah. You eat as much as I do and you *never* gain weight."

"But I'm too *thin*," said Norah. She squinted at a gull soaring against the dazzling blue sky. Fat or thin—what did it matter on such a glorious day? The sun seeped into every pore on her body. Apart from feeling hungry herself, there was nothing she wanted to do except lie here in perfect peace. *This* was what she'd been waiting for all July.

"In a few hours Andrew will be here!" said Janet. "You'll really like him, Norah."

Andrew again! Norah scowled. "How do you *know* I will?"

"Everybody likes Andrew."

When Norah didn't reply, Janet changed the subject. "Don't you have a crush on anyone? Like a movie star or someone? You can share Frankie if you want," she added generously.

"No, I don't!" said Norah crossly. "I don't have to have a crush, you know. It's not a *rule*."

"Well, you don't have to get so mad." Janet sat up and splashed water over her sunburnt legs. "Sometimes I really feel the gap in our ages, Norah. Fourteen is a *lot* different from thirteen."

Norah jumped up and tramped into the trees. She and Janet often quarrelled and it never lasted long, but she wished they hadn't on their first day. She found the tree fort that they had made with Bob and Alec last summer and climbed up to the platform.

I am a lonely shipwrecked sailor, she told herself. My throat is parched and all I have to eat is a few berries …

But she couldn't make it real. That comforting imaginary world of pilots and cowboys and shipwrecked sailors, which she had been able to step into easily for years, suddenly seemed closed to her.

Her stomach rumbled and she started to descend, but the foothold they had nailed to the tree trunk crumbled under her foot. "Oh, *swell*," groaned Norah, pulling herself up to the platform again.

"Help!" she called in mock anguish. "Help me, fair sir! I'm stuck in this tree and a dragon is coming!"

Janet rushed through the woods and they couldn't stop laughing as she helped Norah down, Bosley barking and jumping around them. All the way back to Gairloch they made each other start up again, as they kept on pretending to pretend.

AFTER LUNCH Norah read for a while on her rock, until she got too hot. Then she wandered down to feel the water, wondering whether an hour had passed since she had eaten and it would be safe to swim without getting cramps.

Aunt Mary was standing on the dock, all dressed up in a print dress and a yellow straw hat. Her hair, usually rolled into a tight knot, was in loose waves around her face. "Oh, Norah, I was looking for you. Gerald told me you passed your test with flying colours. Would you take me over to the mainland? Mr. Hancock has to pick up Andrew later and I need to go to Port Schofield."

"Sure!" They settled themselves in the *Putt-Putt* and Norah, flushed with importance, backed it carefully out of its slip. Flo and Janet and Clare were always driving the Elders somewhere; now she could too.

Aunt Mary sat in the bow beside her, clutching her hat. Her cheeks were pink and she looked unusually animated.

"Why are you going to Port Schofield?" Norah asked. "Should I wait for you? Then I could take you back."

"Um … I think it would be best if I went alone, Norah. I have an appointment that might take a long time, and you'll want to be there when Andrew arrives. I'll be finished before dinner—could you come and pick me up at five-thirty?"

She waved goodbye from the dock and hurried away. Norah wondered why she didn't carry her usual shopping basket.

On the way back she went as fast as she dared, bouncing the launch on the waves and getting drenched. She slowed down sedately when she was within view of the island. Gavin, Sally, Peter and Ross were sitting in a row on the dock, each dangling a line in the water.

"Look at all the bass we've caught, Norah!" Gavin showed her a pail full of flopping silver fish.

Norah fetched a fishing pole from the boathouse and joined them. They caught four more bass, cleaned them in the lake and took them up to Hanny to put in the icehouse. Then they all went swimming. The water was so warm now that they stayed in until the tips of their fingers became wrinkled.

"This summer we're being detectives," Gavin told Norah as they baked on their towels in the burning sun. "We have an agency called 'The Fearless Four.'"

"We'll solve *anything*," said Sally. "No case is too difficult."

"Peter and I got a fingerprinting set for Christmas last year," said Ross.

"And I borrowed Aunt Florence's magnifying glass," said Gavin.

"So what case are you solving right now?" asked Norah lazily.

"We haven't actually *begun* yet," Gavin told her. "We're getting prepared, though. Tonight we're going to take everyone's fingerprints, so we'll have them on record."

"Our headquarters are in the playhouse," said Peter. "No one else seems to be using it this year," he added defensively. Last summer the younger cousins had been banned from the playhouse by the Hornets.

Gavin looked worried. "Is that all right, Norah? We've already moved some stuff in there."

"Go ahead and use it," Norah told them.

"Thanks!" said Sally. "If you want anything solved, just come and see us there."

Norah promised she would. She'd never thought of playing detective herself. Now it was too late.

At two-thirty Mr. Hancock, Flo and Janet took off in the *Florence* to pick up Andrew in Port Clarkson. Two hours later most of the clan were on the dock waiting for them to come back. Norah hadn't intended to meet him with the others, but curiosity kept her there.

"He's here! Andrew! Andrew!" screamed Clare, waving both arms.

"For heaven's sake, Clare, control yourself!" Aunt Mar told her daughter. But Clare shrieked even louder when the launch drew up to the dock. A tall boy stepped out, laughing as he pushed away Clare's attacking arms.

"My dear boy, how wonderful to have you back with us." Everyone let Aunt Florence greet him next, then they all descended upon him. Andrew didn't seem to mind. He shook hands with his uncles and kissed his aunts' cheeks, his deep laugh rising above the babble.

He acts like he's a prince or someone, Norah thought.

"You've never met our war guests, have you?" said Aunt Florence. Norah scanned Andrew's face warily as she and Gavin were introduced. He had slicked-back, wavy brown hair, a wide mouth and long grey eyes that curled up at the edges and made him look as if he were always smiling. Norah frowned. Anyone this good-looking was bound to be conceited.

Andrew focused his smile on her and said quietly, "How are you, Norah? I've heard a lot about you. Do you feel like a Canadian now that you've been here for so long?"

How dare he ask something so personal! He'd only just met her! And he acted so condescending, as if he felt sorry for her. Norah didn't answer. She moved away as Andrew, hemmed in by his relatives, was practically carried up to the cottage.

Norah stayed down at the dock with her book until it was time to pick up Aunt Mary, trying not to hear the whoops of laughter from above. Her first day back had turned sour. And the rest of the summer was going to be terrible if all this fuss over Andrew continued. But maybe he wouldn't stay long.

"Has he come?" asked Aunt Mary as soon as Norah landed at the Port Schofield dock. Norah nodded curtly.

"Isn't he nice? Do you like him? I think there's something really special about Andrew."

Norah kept her face straight ahead, trying to conceal her scowl.

4

Andrew

$\mathcal{A}$fter the children's dinner Norah took out the canoe. The steady pull of the paddle soothed her jangled feelings and she pretended she was the only person on the lake. But just as she came back around the corner of Little Island she heard Gavin calling her. Every evening the whole family had to gather in the living room for games and reading aloud.

Gavin waited while Norah lifted up the canoe. "Did you know Andrew once caught a lake trout that was as big as *Denny*?" he told her.

"That's impossible," snapped Norah.

She lingered in the doorway of the living room, looking for Andrew so she could sit as far away from him as possible. He was on one side of the fireplace, Denny on his lap and the rest of the cousins as close to him as they could get. Gavin skipped over to join them.

Aunt Bea leaned towards Andrew, an eager look on her foolish face. "Now tell us about your mother. Is she over that dreadful flu?"

"It wasn't flu, it was a cold," said Aunt Florence.

"It was flu!" cried Aunt Bea, her hair falling out of its pins. "She told us in her last letter!"

"It was a cold," Aunt Florence repeated firmly. "You know you never read letters properly, Bea—you must make up things you *think* you've read."

"I certainly do not!"

"Now, now, you two," interrupted Uncle Reg. "Why don't you ask Andrew? Surely *he* knows."

Andrew had been throwing amused glances at Flo. "I think it was … a kind of flu-y cold," he said carefully. "And she's fine now."

"Do you want to come sailing with Gerald and me tomorrow, Andrew?" Flo asked him.

"Sure! I wonder if I remember how. But you two are such experts, you can show me what to do."

"Can I come?" Clare asked.

"And me?" said Janet and Peter at the same time.

"We'll let Andrew get used to the boat again, then you can each have a turn," said Uncle Gerald.

Andrew glanced all the way across the room at Norah, who had been staring at him. She quickly lowered her eyes.

"Do you like sailing, Norah?"

"Not much," she shrugged.

"But you *love* sailing!" Gavin gave his sister a puzzled look, then said to Andrew, "I like sailing and I don't take up very much room."

Andrew laughed. "Then you can be our first passenger."

"Tell us about university," said Uncle Gerald. "You're taking COTC classes along with your regular engineering course, right? How soon can you be an officer?"

"In a few years," said Andrew.

"I certainly envy you. If it wasn't for these darned eyes ..."

"It must have been frustrating for you, being turned down," said Andrew quietly.

"Well I'm certainly kept busy. It was difficult to take this month off."

"Did you know Gerald left his law firm to be an aircraft assembly inspector, Andrew?" said Aunt Bea proudly.

"But it's not the real thing," said Uncle Gerald. He fingered the small button he always wore on his lapel. "And even if they gave me this, people don't realize that I was turned down. You should hear some of the comments I get, from complete strangers!"

Norah had never seen his placid face look so agitated. Aunt Anne took his arm. "Never mind about them. *We* know you would be fighting if you could."

"If I was young, I wouldn't go on any officer training scheme," said Uncle Barclay gruffly. "I'd join up now! After all, with the Russian victory and the Americans finally in on it, the tide's beginning to turn. You may not even get over there, Andrew."

Aunt Dorothy gave her husband a horrified look. "Oh no, Barclay! Andrew's only nineteen—he's too young to go now." She shuddered. "It will be a blessing if he doesn't have to at all—and I'm glad you couldn't, Gerald."

"I was nineteen," Uncle Barclay reminded her.

The colour had left Andrew's cheeks, and a muscle twitched in one of them. "Perhaps you're right, Uncle Barclay," he said slowly. "But Mother is determined that I become an officer."

"She's perfectly right," said Aunt Florence briskly. "There's no reason you should join up as a common soldier. But let's have no more depressing talk about the war. Tell us what your family has been up to, Andrew."

Norah had joined Janet in a game of cribbage. She tried to shut her ears to Andrew, but he was such a good storyteller she couldn't help listening. He was describing his mother's new volunteer work driving an ambulance. Every time Norah stole a glance at him she noticed how his long hands gesticulated every word: pointing, turning and slicing through the air as if he were conducting music.

"You're not paying attention, Norah!" complained Janet. "I said go!"

Before the younger children were sent to bed, Aunt Florence took out her book. This week it was *The Wind in the Willows*. Norah had to admit that Aunt Florence was the best reader she'd ever heard. She sank into the story with relief. Andrew was also listening intently, a delighted smile on his face.

"Bravo for Toad!" he cried at the end of the chapter. "I remember you reading that when I was about six, Aunt Florence."

Andrew got down on the floor, held up his arms as if clutching a steering wheel, and stuck his legs straight out in front of him. "Poop-poop!" he muttered faintly. "Poop-poop!" The younger cousins collapsed with giggles.

"My dear boy," said Aunt Florence. "I'd forgotten what a good actor you are."

"Are you doing many plays?" Aunt Catherine asked.

"As many as I can!" said Andrew. "I was Prince Henry in our college production of *Henry IV* this year."

He stood up and looked at them silently for a second, his graceful body suddenly regal. His cheek twitched again and, when he spoke, his words were both disdainful and wistful:

> *Yet herein will I imitate the sun,*
> *Who doth permit the base contagious clouds*
> *To smother up his beauty from the world,*
> *That, when he please again to be himself,*
> *Being wanted, he may be more wonder'd at ...*

He stopped abruptly, his face flushed. All the family applauded at how easily he had changed from being a conceited toad to a courtly prince.

All except Norah. *Show-off,* she muttered under her breath.

"HAVEN'T THEY COME back from sailing yet?" Janet asked the next morning. She and Clare and Norah were doing their laundry together at the back of the cottage.

Norah didn't answer. She concentrated on scrubbing her blouse against the ripply metal of the scrub-board.

This was the only part of being at Gairloch that she disliked. Each of the older girls had to do her own laundry, which meant heating up water, rubbing until your hands ached, and wringing out each piece of clothing to hang up in the sun.

"It's my turn to go in the boat next," said Clare. She shaded her eyes as she gazed out over the lake, then turned to Janet. "Wasn't it awful when your dad said Andrew should be a soldier right now?"

"He couldn't help it," retorted Janet. "That's just the way Dad is. All he ever talks about is the First World War and this one."

"I think Uncle Barclay was right," said Norah. The other two stopped washing and looked at her with astonishment.

"What do you mean?" said Clare coldly.

"I mean, I think Andrew *should* join up now. He's probably just trying to avoid it by going to university. I think he's a coward."

"He's not!" Clare flicked some of her soapy water at Norah. "You have no right to say that about one of our relatives!"

Resisting the urge to dump her whole pail of dirty water over Clare, Norah bent her head down and resumed scrubbing. "I can say what I want," she muttered. "He's not *my* relative. You all treat Andrew as if he was royalty or something."

"Why—you—" But then Clare spotted the sail and ran down the steps.

"You haven't finished your laundry!" Janet called after her. "Now I'll have to do it for her," she grumbled.

Norah could have cried with frustration at being forced into a stupid confrontation with Clare. But she prided herself on *never* crying; she had done too much of it in her first few months in Canada.

Why had she said that about Andrew? The words had rushed out before she'd known if she meant them.

"You're wrong about Andrew," mumbled Janet through a mouthful of clothes-pins. "Why did you say such a mean thing? He hasn't done anything to you. And he's so nice!"

"I don't know," said Norah miserably. "I just— don't—*like* him!" Then she ran away too, leaving Janet to hang up all the clothes by herself.

NORAH HEADED TOWARDS HER ROCK, but on the way she almost collided with Flo.

"I was just looking for you, Norah," said the older girl. "Andrew and I picked up the mail. Here's a letter from England for you!"

Norah clutched the letter as she ran up to her lookout. As always, she took a steadying breath before daring to open it. Bad news usually comes in a telegram, not in a letter, she reminded herself. The envelope was a mess; it had been ripped open and resealed by the censor, and the layers of labels showed how many times it had been used. She squinted in the glaring sun and read.

Dear Norah and Gavin,

Congratulations to both of you on your excellent marks in school! Dad and I are so proud of you. We can't believe you are old enough to be going into "grade four" and "grade eight" this fall. When you are back in England you'll find it strange to say "form" instead of grade.

I must tell you all about Muriel's wedding. Of course we couldn't do anything fancy, but we had a very good time all the same. Muriel and Barry were only able to get a few days' leave, but Barry's mother came all the way from Devon and Tibby managed to get down from Reading for the day to be bridesmaid. After the church ceremony we had a small celebration at the house for just the family. I saved my sugar rations for weeks and the hens have been laying well, so I was able to make a small cake. You never would have guessed I used marge instead of butter. Of course I couldn't ice it, but Tibby put a bunch of sweet peas on top and they looked lovely. Grandad somehow managed to get a bottle of wine and we all drank a toast to the two of you as well as to the bride and groom. Muriel looked beautiful in her pink suit. She cut it out of that old coat of mine. Barry was very handsome in his uniform. He's such a nice boy, I'm sure you'll like him. Muriel promises to send you a snap of him soon.

After our little party we all went off to the dance in the village hall. A lot of American GIs were there and they had everyone doing the jitterbug! Even Dad and I tried it but it wore us out. Grandad wanted to try but I wouldn't let him. As usual he forgets his age.

Yesterday, while I was waiting in the fish queue, I stood next to Mrs. Brown. She said she's having a hard time keeping Joey away from the Americans when they come into the village. He and all the other children run up to them asking "Any gum, chum?" Usually they get some! The village is divided in its feelings about the Americans. Some people, including Grandad, think they're too boastful, but Dad and I find them pleasant and friendly. And after all, look what they're doing for us!

Our pig club has a new pig! So I'm saving scraps for it and Grandad takes them to the pig every evening. He stays and talks to it as if it's a person! It's getting nice and plump and I'm sure it will be as delicious as the last one.

I wrote to Mrs. Ogilvie to thank her for her last parcel, but I'd like to thank both of you as well. I'm sure you helped to pick out the things. You've no idea how grateful we are. The soap was especially appreciated—it's so hard to find. What kind people they are.

Norah, I also wrote to Mrs. Ogilvie and asked her to tell you about a very important matter. I hope she does so soon. It's too personal for a letter.

By the time you get this you will be back from your trip across Canada and enjoying Gairloch again. What lucky children you are! Dad says he hopes you each kept a journal. We are looking forward to hearing about it and so is everyone else in the village. Even after three years, someone asks about you every day.

I must stop this now and dig up some potatoes for dinner. Muriel has introduced me to slacks! They're so comfortable around the house and do save on stockings.

We all send our very best wishes and hope as usual that it won't be too long before you come back to us.

Love from us all,
Mum

Norah thumped the letter so hard against the ground that she grazed her fist.

Their school marks were such old news; why did the mail have to take so long each way? What did Mum ask Aunt Florence to tell her? Surely not the crazy story she *had* told her. Why hadn't she thought of keeping a journal?

Why did Muriel have to *change*? Norah had completely forgotten that her oldest sister was getting married.

Poor Mum, scrimping so much just to make a cake. Norah could always sense the weariness behind her cheerful words.

What if something had happened to them that they weren't telling her about? Why should she and Gavin be safe in Canada when her family was always in danger?

If only she could *be* there, playing cricket with Dad and helping Mum with the chickens. If only she could tell them how much she loved them, but somehow she never could say that in her own letters.

Gradually Norah got control of her racing emotions. After all, she should be used to these letters by now.

She would read the letter to Gavin and answer it tonight; she always liked to get that done before Aunt

Florence reminded her, so that she could say smugly, "I've already written it." But it was going to be especially hard to be cheerful in this one. She couldn't say, "Dear Mum, Dad and Grandad ... At first it was wonderful to get back to Gairloch but a boy has come who has spoiled everything."

Late that afternoon Andrew came up the verandah steps as Norah and Gavin were sitting on them and talking about the letter. "Is your family well?" he asked.

"Uh huh," said Gavin. "My big sister got married!"

"You must miss them very much," said Andrew quietly.

Mr. Hancock came out to the verandah and sounded the dinner gong. "Come on, Gavin," Norah said, taking his hand. "Let's go in."

But Gavin called back, "Hey, Andrew—any gum, chum?"

5

On the Lake

*N*orah sat reading her Agatha Christie mystery on the verandah, curled up in an ancient chair with a canopy over it—the family called it a "glider." Besides her rock, the glider was her next favourite retreat at Gairloch. The verandah was like another room, a neutral zone between the cottage and outdoors. Swinging gently on the creaking chains, she could keep an ear open to whatever was going on inside, and watch all the comings and goings without being too suffocated by the clan. The lacy screen of trees beyond the verandah always made her feel secure, as if she were in an airy cave.

But this afternoon she couldn't concentrate on *The Murder of Roger Ackroyd.* The verandah was dotted with other members of the family. From around one corner drifted the usual flow of gossip.

"But what was *her* name?" Aunt Dorothy was asking.

"Wasn't she a Ferguson? The Manitoba Fergusons, not the Ontario ones. Her mother would have been a Baxter," pronounced Aunt Florence. The aunts seemed to know the last names of everyone in all of Canada.

The strains of one of Uncle Reg's Gilbert and Sullivan records floated from around the other corner: "... and his *sisters* and his *cousins* and his *sisters* and his *cousins* and his *aunts*!" Uncle Reg would be stretched out as usual on a chaise longue, close enough to his phonograph to reach over and wind it up.

Aunt Catherine was sitting in a rocking chair not far from Norah, her tiny foot bobbing to the music and her nose in a book. She'd given Norah a friendly wave when she first sat down, but *she* understood that people didn't want to be disturbed when they were reading.

Norah had watched Aunt Bea and Aunt Mar set out for the gazebo, carrying a basket, a kettle and a spirit-lamp. She knew Aunt Anne was at the babies' beach with George and Denny. Now she saw Aunt Mary, again dressed up, descend the steps to the dock. Flo came out of the Girls' Dorm and they both got into the *Putt-Putt* and drove away. Once again Aunt Mary had no shopping bag.

Norah watched the launch disappear, then looked for the sail. By now Andrew and Uncle Gerald, or he and Flo, had taken all the cousins out in the sailboat—everyone but Norah.

Gavin was right—she loved sailing. Two summers ago she and Janet rigged up the rowboat with an improvised sail made out of an old sheet and pretended it was the *Swallow,* from one of Norah's favourite books. But the rowboat was too heavy to move very fast without oars.

They were only allowed to go out in the sailboat when Uncle Gerald or Uncle Peter, Clare's father, was here. But the two youngest uncles were never able to come to Gairloch for long and the other two didn't like sailing.

Now Norah watched Andrew and Uncle Gerald tack as they approached the dock. Gavin and Sally were crouched between them. Norah wanted to be in the boat so much she could feel the jibsheet between her hands.

But she wouldn't ask—not Andrew. She swung the glider violently until its creaking almost drowned out Uncle Reg's record.

"Norah!" Gavin had rushed up the hill to the verandah. He always knew where to find his sister. He climbed into the glider beside her, his cheeks flushed and his fair hair in a tangle. "Did you see me out there? It was swell! We went really fast and I leaned right over the water— that's called 'hiking.' Sally almost forgot to duck when Uncle Gerald gybed. Do you know what gybing is?"

"Of course I do," sighed Norah.

"Andrew sent me to find you," continued Gavin. "He wants to know if you want a turn next. This will be their last sail today."

Despite the reluctance in her mind, Norah's feet seemed to stroll down to the dock on their own. She tried not to let her face show how much she wanted to get into the boat.

"There you are, Norah!" Andrew was sitting in the stern. "You're certainly hard to find. Every time we tried to give you a turn you'd disappeared."

"Want to come now?" Uncle Gerald asked her.

"Yes, please." Norah looked only at Uncle Gerald as she answered. With him along, she could ignore Andrew. She put on a life-jacket and stepped into the *Christina*. The boat's canvas sails crackled in the breeze, as if it were impatient at having to stand still.

"Gerald!" Aunt Anne came hurrying down the steps, Denny in her arms. "Will you come and cope with George? I've left him screaming in the cabin. He says you promised to take him fishing right after lunch and he *won't* mind me. You have to come."

Uncle Gerald frowned. "But we were just about to take Norah for a sail. Can't he wait an hour?"

"You know how worked up he gets. Please, Gerald— I can't do a thing with him!"

"Georgie's screamin' real loud," said Denny with satisfaction. They could all hear the faint, enraged cry: *"Daddy ..."*

"All right ..." Uncle Gerald stepped out of the boat. "Norah's used to sailing, Andrew, and you're doing fine. I think the two of you will be all right on your own." He hurried up to the cabin.

"Let's get going!" said Andrew. He handed Norah the jibsheet and took hold of the mainsheet and the tiller. "Cast us off, Gavin."

Norah thought of leaping from the boat but it was too late. Gavin untied the painter and she had to catch it. Then he pushed away the bow and in an instant she was out on the lake, trapped with Andrew.

Frantically Norah tried to remember her duties as

crew: pulling in the fluttering jibsail and setting it to the same angle as the mainsail. She clutched the rope so tightly, her bones showed through her knuckles. If she had to be in the boat with Andrew, at least she would show him she knew how to sail.

They were going to be too busy to have a conversation. Andrew's only words came every few minutes: "Ready about ... tacking." At first the two of them moved awkwardly, stumbling over each other's legs; but soon they synchronized their movements and shifted from one side of the boat to the other as one person. The *Christina* skimmed the water like a gull, the wake curling behind. No motor noise jarred the ride, just the vibration of the wind against the taut sails. Norah gazed up the mast, which seemed to pierce the bright sky. Then they hiked out to flatten the boat and she leaned far over the water, her hair whipping backwards and spray flying into her mouth. She let her mind fill with the joy of sailing, and pretended there was no one in the boat but her.

Finally Andrew, shaking the water out of his hair, grinned at her. "I hate to end this, but I think we'll have to go back. I missed lunch and I'm ravenous! Get ready to gybe." He reversed the tiller and hauled in the mainsheet. "Boom over ..."

Norah ducked her head as the boom swung across. Now the two sails billowed out on either side and the *Christina* became a sedate swan swimming for shore.

Andrew pulled up the centreboard and told Norah to move back. She perched on one side so she'd be as far away from him as possible. She tried to keep watching the jib, but there wasn't much need to concentrate on it now that they were moving more slowly.

Andrew stretched out his long legs and leaned against the stern. "You're a good sailor, Norah. Did you learn in England?"

Why did he always have to look right into her face when he talked to her? Norah's words came out in hard, painful chunks. "Oh, no. *My* family doesn't own any boats. I learned here. Uncle Gerald taught me. And Uncle Peter."

"I learned at Gairloch, too. My dad taught me—my first dad, that is. But my stepfather doesn't like sailing. He gets seasick!"

Norah wondered if he liked his stepfather and how he had felt when his mother married again. But if she asked him that he might ask *her* more questions.

It was so difficult to remain aloof when they were sharing something so enjoyable. Norah trailed one hand in the warm water. Perhaps—just for this trip—she would let herself forget about how much he bothered her.

"Your little brother is a real character," chuckled Andrew. "He told us that his elephant—what does he call it—Creature?—should have a life-jacket too, in case he fell in. He must have been very young when he left England."

"He was five," said Norah. "That's the youngest age you could come over on the overseas evacuation plan." For a surprised second she wondered if her parents would have sent her alone if Gavin had been only four.

"At least you had each other," said Andrew, as if he were reading her thoughts. "And did you really not know who you'd be living with? Aunt Florence said you were *assigned* to her!"

"No, we didn't know. We waited for a week at the university before we found out."

"I'm not sure *I'd* like to have Aunt Florence as my guardian," said Andrew. "Aunt Mary is a peach, but Aunt Florence has always reminded me of the Queen of Hearts in *Alice*—'Off with her head!' She read *Alice* to us the last summer I was here with my parents. That book sometimes reminds me of this whole family. A bit mad, don't you think?"

Norah nodded vigorously, remembering Aunt Florence's odd story about the little visitor. "Sometimes I just don't understand them! And Aunt Florence *is* hard to live with. She's so fussy!" Then, remembering as always that she was a guest in this country, Norah added dutifully, "But it was very kind of her to take us in. And sometimes she's funny. Last winter she took up tap dancing! They had lessons on the radio and she thought it would be good for her figure. Gavin and I used to spy on her. She looked *so* silly, bouncing around the dining room. But she gave up after two lessons—she said it was bad for her heart."

Andrew threw back his head and crowed with laughter. "Aunt Florence probably has a better heart than *I* have! She can be ridiculous, but there's something magnificent about her, too. I think my grandmother was terrified of her. Did you know this boat was named after her?"

"After who?"

"My grandmother. Christina. She was Aunt Florence's younger sister, but she and my grandfather are both dead. She was my father's mother—and Aunt Dorothy's and Uncle Peter's."

"Oh." Sorting out the Drummonds was like doing a hard puzzle.

Andrew sighed. "My grandparents were easy to take, but I think my mother was glad to get away from the rest of the family when she married again. Yet there's something endearing about all of them, too. When I'm here I feel so ... *safe*. As if nothing has changed and nothing else in the world—the war especially—exists. I guess that's why I have to come back once in a while. And of course the best part is this incredible lake—just look at it!"

Andrew let go of the tiller and flung his arms dramatically. The boom swung over without warning, the boat heeled—and Norah was tipped backwards into the water.

She heard herself yelp before she went under. But she bobbed up immediately like a cork, spluttering out a huge mouthful of the lake. The *Christina* was making a wide circle ahead of her as it turned back.

When the boat drew up beside her, Andrew leaned over and grabbed the back of her life-jacket. He fished her out, dripping and giggling. "Norah, are you all right? What a *stupid* thing to do—I'm so sorry!"

"I'm okay," gasped Norah. "I fell off before the boom could hit me. It was just such a surprise! But the water isn't cold at all. At least you righted the boat before it capsized."

"You're shivering! Here, take this off." Andrew helped her undo her sopping life-jacket, and rubbed her arms and legs. Then he took off his shirt and wrapped it tightly around her, his face full of concern. "Don't tell anyone about this, promise? Think of what Aunt Florence would say, nearly drowning her war guest! I still can't believe I did something so idiotic. Don't worry about the jib any more. Just sit up on the side and get some sun. We're almost there—I can see the dock. I only hope no one saw *us*!"

Norah kept shaking, but it wasn't from being cold. She turned away from Andrew so he couldn't see her face and struggled to get herself under control. With awe, she hugged his protecting shirt around her, still feeling the touch of his warm hands on her skin.

6

Secrets

Norah left Andrew without a word. Up in the boathouse she peeled off her wet clothes and put on dry ones, then hurried out again in a daze, not knowing where she was going.

"Can you help me?" Flo's words startled Norah. She was plodding down the steps, weighed down by Uncle Reg's phonograph. Norah ran up and grabbed one end of it.

"Where are you taking this?" she asked.

"To the boathouse!" said Flo triumphantly. "It's for us! The Elders have a new one—Mr. Hancock just picked it up in Port Clarkson. Uncle Reg says this one sounds tinny, but I don't care. Now we can have music!"

Flo began setting up the phonograph on Sally's empty bed—the little girl had got her way and now slept in the Boys' Dorm. Janet and Clare rushed in, their arms full of records. "Where is it?" asked Clare. "Dibs on choosing first! I wondered when I'd get to play these—Uncle Reg was always hogging it."

She dropped her pile of records on the bed and flipped

through them. "Put on this one—it's number one on the hit parade."

Frank Sinatra's smooth voice filled the space. The sound *was* tinny and the needle scratched, but having music made the boathouse even cosier. Each of the girls curled up on her bed and hummed along.

"You'll never know just how much I care …"

That's *me*! thought Norah. Turning to the wall to hide her blushing cheeks she mouthed, "I love you." The revelation was still a shock—like bursting out of her old skin and finding a fragile new one underneath.

Every Saturday in the city Norah went to the movies with her friends. Now she felt as if *she* were in a movie: like *Casablanca* or *Gone with the Wind.*

Her feelings had to be a secret; even—especially— from Andrew. She didn't know how she would handle it if he knew. For now she just wanted to think about him as much as possible.

The song ended and Clare beat Janet to the turntable and started it again. Flo jumped up and grabbed her brush. "How I wish I could *do* something!" she grumbled, dragging the bristles through her long hair.

"What do you mean?" asked Janet.

"I wish I could leave school and get a job in an airplane factory or something—but Mother and Dad won't let me. It's so unfair. All my male friends are over there helping to fight and I'm stuck at home learning *algebra*."

"The war's so boring," yawned Clare. "How can you be interested in it?"

"I don't see why I can't contribute," said Flo. "Like Norah's older sisters—they're in the British army, right, Norah? As soon as I'm eighteen I'm going to join the RCAF, if I can talk Mother and Dad into it. But that's a whole year away. Lucky Andrew—at least he's starting his officer training this fall."

"Is Andrew staying for the rest of summer?" asked Norah. She dropped his name into the conversation as casually as she could, amazed that it didn't ring out like a gong to the others the way it did to her.

"I think he's staying until university starts," said Janet. "So he'll probably drive back to Toronto with you."

"Too bad for Norah," said Clare. "You'll just have to put up with him."

"Don't you like Andrew?" Flo asked her with surprise.

Norah flushed so hotly she was sure Flo guessed her secret. But Clare saved her. "Norah's too much of a tomboy to like boys. When we're all engaged she'll still be climbing trees."

"Don't be mean, Clare," said Flo. "There's no reason Norah has to be interested in boys. She's only thirteen— give her time." She smiled at Norah, and Norah was so relieved she smiled back. Let them all go on thinking she didn't like Andrew.

The record ended and the rasp of the needle filled the room. Janet put on "That Old Black Magic" and Norah lay back dreamily. She had never really listened to the song; now every word seemed to be speaking to her alone.

"NORAH, WAIT!" called Janet the next morning. "I thought we were going out in the canoe!"

But Norah had already fled to her rock. She lay on her stomach and peered down at the cabins. In front of the larger one Aunt Anne was shaking out a rug, shooing away George and Denny, who were playing with toy cars on the front steps.

Andrew's cabin looked unoccupied. But he must be in there because he hadn't been to breakfast yet. If he came out, could she call him and wave casually? She knew she couldn't. Right now she just wanted to study him—to learn him by heart.

But in that case she'd better hide, in case he looked up and saw her here. At the back of Andrew's cabin were some low-lying bushes. Norah waited until Aunt Anne went inside, taking the little boys with her. Then she slipped off the rock and ran down to hide in the bushes.

Whew! Her heart thudded as she crouched in the damp dirt. The branches poked into her back, and she wanted to sneeze from the dry leafy smell. Immediately, she wished she hadn't come; it would be so humiliating if Andrew discovered her. But now that she was here, it was safer to stay hidden until he came out.

She didn't have long to wait. The screen door creaked and slammed and she peeked out to see Andrew stroll out of the cabin and up the hill to the main cottage. When he was far enough away, she dashed back up to her rock and watched his progress.

He wore a white shirt that emphasized his tan, and khaki shorts. His hair glistened in the sun. Norah sighed, thinking of all the days she had wasted avoiding him when she could have been feasting her eyes like this. Andrew went in the kitchen door—Norah could hear him greeting Hanny before it closed.

For the next few days she tracked Andrew as much as possible, feeling as daring and resourceful as when she had been ten, watching for enemy paratroopers during the Battle of Britain. Janet complained because she couldn't find her. "What are you *doing* by yourself so much?"

"Oh … reading." Norah carried a book as an alibi and often needed it while she waited for Andrew to emerge from the cabin or return from the mainland. The lake was too calm for sailing and he spent some time off the island—she'd heard him say he was visiting friends.

"Reading …" sighed Janet. "I wish you'd do something with *me*, Norah. Clare's always reading too—movie magazines. Or she's visiting her friend Louise on Cliff Island. And Flo spends all her time writing letters. I'm so *bored*! Gairloch used to be a lot more fun than it has been this summer. I thought that would change when you came."

Norah squirmed at her foster cousin's forlorn expression. "Okay—let's go out in the rowboat." They rowed out to the middle of the lake and spent an hour diving off the boat. But all the time, Norah wondered what Andrew was up to.

Every night in bed, and during her solitary vigils during the day, Norah made up elaborate stories about her and Andrew. Sometimes she didn't have on her life-jacket when she had fallen out of the boat and he rescued her just before she drowned. Sometimes she rescued *him*, pulling him to shore and applying mouth-to-mouth resuscitation.

"You are the one," he would say when his eyes finally opened. "The special person I've been waiting for all my life." Because of Norah's age they had to keep their love hidden. Andrew would meet Norah secretly in Toronto during his time at university. Then he would go away to war carrying her picture in his pocket. He would be a hero and win many medals. After the war, when she was eighteen, he would return and marry her. (This part needed adjusting because Norah didn't want the war to go on that long.) *They would live in England, in the same village as her parents. Aunt Florence would be furious that Norah had married so young, but there was nothing she could do ...*

She picked up a sharp stone and began scratching initials in the rock: N.S. + A.D.

"Ugh!" A wet nose was poking the back of her neck. Then Bosley slobbered all over her face. Gavin was climbing up the rock behind him.

"What are you doing, Norah?"

Quickly Norah moved so she was sitting on top of the initials. She smiled at her brother.

"Nothing much. How's the detective agency?"

"Okay ... but we haven't got any *cases*. Uncle Reg hired us to find his glasses but that was too easy—they were on the verandah, where he always leaves them."

Norah gazed out at the lake and saw Janet returning in the *Putt-Putt* with Aunt Mary. "I know what you can investigate," she said.

"What?"

"You can find out why Aunt Mary has gone into Port Schofield almost every day since we got here."

"I heard Aunt Florence ask her that—she's getting a dress made. There's a lady there who sews."

"That's what she says, but I don't think that's *all* she does. On Friday I got there early to pick her up and I saw her coming from that big hotel across from the marina—running! Then she went over the bridge and came out from the direction of the dressmaker's as if she'd been there all along. And yesterday I saw her coming *out* of the hotel when I drove the boat by it—she had her head down and didn't see me."

"Wow!" said Gavin. "I wonder what she was doing there? See you later, Norah!" Gavin sped off to tell his gang.

Norah went back to her scratching, glad she had given him something to do. She felt vaguely curious about Aunt Mary, but she was sure there was some boring explanation. Aunt Mary was too ordinary to be involved in a real mystery.

All of her senses were alert when she spotted Andrew come out of his cabin, walk to the lake and dive into the water, swimming vigorously to Little Island.

Norah wiped back her sticky hair and sighed. She felt dopey, as if she couldn't wake up. A swim would refresh her; but she couldn't go down while he was still there.

A few times since their sail Andrew had tried to talk to Norah. She mumbled her answers, too shy about her new feelings to have a conversation. He seemed to realize she didn't want to talk, and, although he sometimes gave her a quizzical look, he left her alone. That was the way she wanted it; for the time being, anyhow.

BEFORE THE CHILDREN'S DINNER that evening Norah sat in the living room with her book. She was actually reading it; Andrew and Flo had left the island to go to a dance at Bala.

"And what are you doing in a corner all by yourself?" Uncle Barclay had come into the room without her noticing; he was pinning up little flags onto a huge world map he'd hung on the wall near the piano.

Norah shrugged. "Just reading." She went over to examine his map. Most of the countries bristled with markers, according to some complicated scheme of Uncle Barclay's that she didn't understand.

"What's that place?" she asked politely, pointing to a small green island that he was covering with flags.

"Sicily," said Uncle Barclay with satisfaction. "We're making great advances there—it's very encouraging."

"Do you think we'll *win* the war?" Norah asked him, still staring at the flags dotted all over the map. She hadn't realized how much of the world it now affected.

"Of course we'll win! It's looking better all the time— the Axis can't hold out forever."

Uncle Barclay knew more about the war than anyone

else; perhaps he could help her make her daydreaming more accurate. "How long do you think it will be before Andrew is in it?" she asked carefully, thrilling as usual at pronouncing his name.

"Well, he just might get in at the end of it. Then again, he could miss it entirely. That's what I don't understand. If *I* was younger and could help fight that brute …" Uncle Barclay snorted, then looked at her kindly. "The only bad thing about the Allies winning is that then you and Gavin will have to go back to England. Flo and Janet will certainly miss you. So will we all," he added gruffly. "But you'll be glad to see your family. Aunt Florence told us how homesick you were at first—you must still miss them."

Norah gave him a smile in exchange for his own awkward one. Uncle Barclay was much stiffer than clownish Uncle Reg, but he was nice in his own way. Guiltily she realized that, this week especially, her thoughts had never been farther from England. If someone told her she could go home tomorrow she wasn't sure she'd want to— not if it meant leaving Andrew.

THAT NIGHT she couldn't sleep. She crept past her inert roommates to go out and sit on the dock. The smaller launch was still gone; Andrew and Flo hadn't come back yet.

Someone coughed and Norah jerked her head around. To her surprise she saw Aunt Mary standing on the far end of the dock, her cigarette a tiny glow in the darkness. She came over and sat beside Norah.

"What are you doing up?" she smiled. "Couldn't you sleep either?"

Norah shook her head. For a few comfortable moments they gazed at the moon. One side of it was caved in, as if someone had taken a bite out of it. Strands of mist rose from the lake like steam. In the distance a dog barked, then was silent.

"It's so quiet up here this summer," said Aunt Mary. "I guess some people have shut up their cottages until after the war. I have an idea." Aunt Mary jumped up, sounding as young as Norah. "Let's take the canoe to Little Island!"

"Now?" Norah could hardly believe what she was hearing. Timid Aunt Mary suggesting such an adventure?

"Why not? Go and get a sweater—it will be cool on the water."

In a few minutes they were in the canoe. At first their dripping paddles made the only sound. Then, by an unspoken agreement, they both began Indian paddling, turning and sliding their blades so they didn't break the surface; then there was no sound at all. In the darkness the shoreline seemed to slip by much faster than it did in daylight. Two summers ago, when she'd first learned how to paddle, Norah had spent hours in this canoe with Aunt Mary.

Little Island made a dark shadow in the water ahead of them. "Shall we get out?" Norah asked shyly. Her voice seemed to boom out in the quiet. Tonight Aunt Mary was a stranger; Norah couldn't predict what she'd want to do next.

"Yes, land over there. I want to show you something."
They pulled the canoe up onto the same logs where
Norah and Janet had sunbathed last week. Then they stole
through the woods to the centre of the island, Aunt
Mary's flashlight beaming their way. Norah took her
hand, feeling as if she were in a dream.

"Here we are!" The flashlight picked out a clump of
six birches that formed a circle. Aunt Mary sat down in
the middle and laughed softly. "Come in, Norah! I haven't
been here for years and years. This was my special place
when I was young. Whenever Mother was upset with me,
I would take refuge over here."

"*We* used to pretend this was a teepee," Norah told
her, cross-legged beside her on the rocky ground. It didn't
feel quite right for one of the Elders to be in the circle
now, even if she had come here as a girl. And it was odd
to be sitting here in the middle of the night in her
pyjamas. She waited; Aunt Mary seemed lit up with
importance, as if she were going to tell Norah something.

"I had a difficult time as a girl, Norah," she said
slowly. "What with my brother's death, then Father's,
and Mother being so ... well, you know how she is. And
then ... I met someone I liked very much. So much that
I wanted to marry him."

Norah's ears stretched. Hanny had once told her that
Aunt Mary had a Secret Sorrow. Now she was finally
going to hear about it!

"Why didn't you?" she asked softly, trying not to stem
the flow of confidence.

"For a number of reasons ..." Aunt Mary's voice grew tender. "His name was Thomas and he was a stockbroker in Toronto. I met him at a church meeting and he began coming over for Sunday dinners. I think Mother liked him; he was respectable enough, even for her. But then he found out he was going to be transferred to Regina."

So Aunt Mary had once been in love too! "Did he *ask* you to marry him?"

"Yes, he did. It took me a week to decide. But finally, after talking it over with Mother, I said no. I just couldn't leave her alone, you see—not after the losses she'd already had. I even asked Thomas if she could come with us, but he was very reluctant to have her. I don't blame him, and Mother didn't want to leave Toronto anyway."

"But that's terrible!" cried Norah. "You gave up the man you loved for *Aunt Florence*? How could you? She ruined your life!"

Aunt Mary patted Norah's hand. "It seemed the right thing to do at the time. And I haven't suffered *that* much, you know. I did then, but I got over it and I think I have a very pleasant life—certainly more pleasant than most people in the world. Think of how much some of them must be suffering in the war this very moment, while we're enjoying this beautiful place."

Sometimes Aunt Mary was too good to be true. Norah crumpled a strip of birchbark and flung it across the clearing. "Think of *you*! Think of Thomas! It's *terrible* that you gave him up!"

"Well, it was all a long time ago and it's over now. And who knows? Maybe I wouldn't have had such a happy life with Thomas. When you grow up you'll find that you have to learn to live with your own decisions." Her voice had a sad, dreamy quality to it, but then she looked up at Norah and laughed. "Well! I don't know why I'm telling you about it. It's just such a restless kind of night. For some reason it made me think of him and I couldn't sleep."

As they paddled back, Norah seethed with the injustice of Aunt Mary's decision. But she had to admit that Aunt Mary herself didn't seem to be upset about it; in fact she was curiously happy and excited. They kissed goodnight, grinning at the secret of their shared expedition.

I'll never give up Andrew for *anyone,* Norah thought sleepily as she crawled back into her warm bed. She tried to stay awake long enough to hear him come in, but when she turned over again it was morning.

7

An Accident

The whole family was assembled on the dock the next afternoon. Norah lay on her stomach, basking after her fifth swim. Lazily she watched Aunt Florence and Aunt Catherine taking what they called their "constitutional."

Aunt Catherine was amazingly spry for someone in her eighties. Her wiry body moved through the water as easily as Norah herself, as she performed her usual ten strokes out and ten strokes in. Bosley accompanied her all the way.

Aunt Florence didn't really swim. Her figure was encased in a ballooning flowered bathing suit she called her "swimming costume" and her head was wrapped in a kind of turban. She let herself awkwardly down the ladder, then heaved herself in, flopping about and spewing water like a whale. Then she emerged, as proud as if she had swum a marathon. All the children suppressed giggles behind their towels.

Denny jumped in again and again, buoyed up by his life-jacket. George was having a swimming lesson. Uncle

Gerald stood at the edge of the dock and held him up by a rope tied around his middle. "Thatta boy! You're doing fine!" he called. The little boy splashed and kicked valiantly. All the other cousins bobbed around him.

Aunt Mary sat in the shade under the roofed part of the dock, deep in a new book called *The Robe*. Uncle Reg sat in the sun, a knotted white handkerchief draped on top of his bald head. He squinted at his needlepoint. This summer he'd asked Aunt Florence to teach him. His sisters teased him but he retorted that he didn't see why a man couldn't be as good at needlepoint as a woman. Now he and Aunt Florence were having a competition to see who could finish a cushion cover first.

Aunt Bea and Aunt Dorothy came down from the changing room that was next to the Girls' Dorm. They sat beside Norah, dangling their feet in the lake and fanning themselves. "I always hate the first plunge," said Aunt Bea. "The only problem with this side of the island is that there's no shore. When I was little I thought there was a sea monster down there!"

Uncle Reg chuckled. "That's because once I dived underneath and grabbed your ankle—do you remember?"

"Of course I do!" bristled Aunt Bea. "It was very naughty and Father was right to punish you."

Norah listened to the two of them bickering as if they were children again. It was so hard to believe that any of the Elders *had* been young.

While everyone was resting after lunch she had made a secret inspection of the cottage walls for pictures of

Andrew. She recognized him in several family groups: a solemn page boy in a kilt at Uncle Gerald's wedding; squeezed between Flo and Clare at a picnic. He didn't look much different when he was Norah's age, though his hair had been lighter and his face not as lean.

If he *were* her age she could be his friend as easily as she was friends with Bernard in the city. Then she wouldn't catch her breath every time she looked at him. Friendship would be much more restful; but there was nothing she could do to stop her love. It *ran* her, as if she were a puppet dangling on its strings.

When she'd found all the pictures of Andrew, Norah turned to a photograph that had been pointed out to her again and again: the first generation of Elders as children, sitting on the steps of the newly built Gairloch. Three sisters and a brother, the girls in white dresses and black stockings. As usual she felt sorry for them, dressed so uncomfortably in the summer. Thirteen-year-old Aunt Florence looked as haughty and confident as she did now. *She* didn't seem to have found it confusing to be a teen-ager. Beside her, in order of age, sat Christina, Bea (pouting) and little Reg, who was smiling mischievously.

On the wall beside Aunt Florence's chair hung a picture of her son, Hugh, who had been killed in World War I. He was standing alone on the verandah, dressed in his uniform. His open, eager face laughed at the camera, as if he could never die.

Norah glanced at a few recent photographs that included her and Gavin. After they left Canada their likenesses would still be hanging here, as if they were really part of the family.

All of the Drummonds, dead and alive, stared at Norah, until she suddenly felt oppressed and fled out to the sunshine.

Now she lifted her head from her towel and watched Andrew and Uncle Gerald race to Little Island and back. When Andrew won, she lowered her face to hide her proud grin. He climbed out and stood over her, puffing and dripping. Norah stiffened and stared at his feet. His long toes were as elegant as his fingers. He dived back into the lake without speaking to her.

Norah flipped over and sighed. It wasn't *enough*. She was no longer content with simply watching Andrew. Now she wished he would talk to her as easily as he had that day in the boat, but her shyness had made him stop paying attention to her. She had to do something to get that attention back.

"Watch me, Norah!" cried Janet. She was poised on the balcony of the boathouse. Then she cannon-balled into the lake; the aunts shrieked in mock alarm as they got splashed.

Norah ran up the stairs to the dorm and climbed out the window to the balcony. For a few seconds she balanced on the railing, curling her toes around it and trying to will Andrew to look at her. She called down to Janet. "Watch *me*! I'm going to dive!"

She had never dived before. It was safe enough—the water was so deep, there was no danger of hitting bottom.

But the lake was an awfully long way below. When Andrew finally glanced up, Norah crouched and sprang.

The lake rushed up at her, then roared in her ears as she shot into its green depths. She struggled up through the watery silence, whooshed out the air from her aching lungs and struck out for the dock. She'd done it!

The family applauded. "Did you see my *sister*?" Gavin asked Ross.

"You're so brave!" said Janet, helping her up the ladder. "I'll never get up the nerve to dive."

"Good for you, Norah," smiled Andrew. "I was much older the first time I did that." His praise rang in her ears for the rest of the day.

THEN NORAH had a much more daring idea than diving off the boathouse. The next morning, after rehearsing the whole scene several times in her head, she walked casually by Andrew's cabin when she knew he was still there. Then she stumbled deliberately. *"Ow!"*

Andrew rushed out. "What's the matter?"

"My ankle," moaned Norah. "I think I twisted it or something. I was just on my way to visit Aunt Anne," she added quickly, so he wouldn't wonder what she'd been doing outside his cabin.

"Let me see." Andrew took Norah's ankle in his hand. He turned it gently in different directions. "Does this hurt?"

"A little—not *too* much." Norah's cheeks flamed. This presence was working too easily; there was something shameful about it.

"Can you stand?" Andrew helped her up and Norah was so overcome with the thrill of having his arms around her that she trembled convincingly.

"It's—it's all right now. I think I can walk on it." She pretended to limp a few steps.

"Come in and rest it for a few minutes. If it doesn't get any better I'll go up and get Aunt Dorothy—she used to be a nurse, you know."

Go *in*, to Andrew's own place? Norah grimaced, not with pain but with excitement, as Andrew helped her through the door and onto a couch.

"Do you want some tea? I've been making my own breakfast in here. It's more peaceful than having it with the Elders. All of them first thing in the morning are too much to take. And Hanny usually gives me leftovers, anyway."

Andrew calling the grown-ups the Elders, as he had in the boat, made Norah feel slightly more at ease. She accepted his offer of tea gratefully; she hadn't had any for ages. Even though children over twelve were allowed tea coupons, Aunt Florence insisted on keeping Norah's for herself and Aunt Mary.

"Toast too?"

"No thanks—I've *had* breakfast."

Andrew toasted bread for himself over the tiny wood stove. Norah looked around the cabin, trying to calm down and savour these precious moments alone with him. She'd been in this cabin a few times before, when various relatives had overflowed from the cottage out here. It was

only one room containing two narrow couches, a table
and chairs, and a shabby rug. Now a large glossy photograph of a handsome man was pinned to one wall.

"Who's that?" Norah dared to ask.

"Laurence Olivier—my inspiration," said Andrew.
"Didn't you ever see him in *Wuthering Heights*? I guess not,
you would have been too young. He's a brilliant actor."

"I thought that was a book."

"The movie was *from* the book."

Norah resolved to borrow it from Aunt Catherine
right away. "Do you think you'll ever be an actor yourself?" she asked timidly. "Aunt Catherine told me she
thinks you should be. She said you were a natural and
she should know—she's seen lots of plays."

"Good old Aunt Catherine," said Andrew. "She's
always taken my acting seriously. Too bad she's the only
one." The muscle jumped in his cheek and his blue-grey
eyes looked sad.

"But everyone thinks you're a *wonderful* actor!" cried
Norah, forgetting her shyness. "You heard what Aunt
Florence said on your first night."

"Yes—as long as it's just a hobby. I'll tell you something, Norah. I *do* want to be an actor. More than
anything in the world. But *they*—all the Elders and especially my mother and stepfather—think I should be an
engineer, like my father. That's what I've been taking at
university and what I'll continue taking at U of T along
with the COTC course. You wouldn't believe how boring it
is. But they don't need actors in the war," he added dryly.

"Can't you become an actor *after* the war?" asked Norah.

"I suppose so. Maybe I'll have the guts to do it by then. You see, it's not just because it's a good lead-in to officer training that they had me take engineering. It's because it's practical and will give me the kind of career every other man in this family has always had—something that will make me lots of money, that will *establish* me ..."

He waved his piece of toast in time to the rise and fall of his words. The bitterness in his voice made Norah uncomfortable. This wasn't how she wanted him to be; he was supposed to be confident and cheerful. "I don't see why you can't be an actor if you want to be," she said impatiently.

She was relieved when Andrew smiled. "You're perfectly right. And I shouldn't be boring you with my problems. I don't know why I'm telling you all this—probably because you're *not* part of the family." He glanced at his watch. "Now ... how's the ankle?"

Norah had completely forgotten she was supposed to have twisted her ankle. "Oh!" she said with surprise. "I guess it's going to be all right." She stood up, put her weight on it, and limped around the room. "Yes, I'm sure it will be. The more I walk on it the better it feels."

"Good." Andrew was gathering up a tennis racquet and a white sweater. He wanted her to go.

"I'm meeting some friends at eleven," he said. "Be sure to get someone to look at your ankle if it bothers you."

"I will." Norah hobbled out of the cabin and up the hill, trying to remember which foot she was supposed to be favouring. She turned back to wave but Andrew was already hurrying to the dock.

Still, he'd asked her in! And he'd confided in her! For the rest of the day Norah moved around in a cloud of happiness, and that evening it was crowned when Andrew asked her in a concerned voice, "Is your ankle better, Norah?"

"Yes, thanks," she said in a croak, as his eyes focused on hers.

"What happened to your ankle, Norah?" demanded Aunt Florence. "Why didn't you tell me?"

"I just twisted it a bit. It's fine now. It doesn't even hurt."

Aunt Florence looked so suspicious that Norah retreated from the room. She still felt guilty about her trick—but it had worked! Surely, from now on, Andrew would pay more attention to her. And, after all, she'd only been in love with him for four days—though it seemed like years. It was natural that he'd take that long to really notice her.

World-famous actor Andrew Drummond says he wouldn't have persisted with his career if it had not been for the encouragement of his beloved wife, Norah. Often compared to Laurence Olivier, this handsome star says he has his wife in mind every time he plays a love scene ...

8

Being Detectives

"Norah, we'd like to have a meeting with you." The Fearless Four stood solemnly on the verandah. "Could you please come to our headquarters?" added Gavin.

Norah left the glider and followed them along the path to the playhouse. Above the door was pinned a sign—FEARLESS FOUR DETECTIVE AGENCY—NO CASE TOO DIFFICULT. Inside, all the evidence of the Hornets had been cleared away. Now a pair of toy handcuffs and a magnifying glass sat on a low table. Leaning against the wall was a chart covered with all the family's fingerprints. A complete set of Sherlock Holmes books stood on a rickety shelf; Creature was perched on top, as if he were guarding all this.

Norah was struck by how small the room was; her arms and legs seemed to fill the whole space. She sat on the floor with the others around the table. "Does Aunt Florence know you have these books out here?" she asked, reaching up to touch one of the red leather bindings.

"Well ... not exactly," said Gavin, always truthful.

"She said I could borrow them, but she thinks they're in the Boys' Dorm. We'll put them back at the end of the summer. Listen, Norah—we need your help."

"What for?"

"We just can't crack this case," said Peter solemnly. He pushed up the thick glasses that were always sliding down his nose.

"*What* case?"

"Aunt Mary's," said Sally impatiently. "We've got a lot of clues but now we're stuck."

Gavin handed Norah his notebook. A pencil was tied by a bedraggled string to a hole in the cover. She opened it to the first page, which was headed "Clues—The Case of the Mysterious Visits."

1. Aunt Mary has gone to Port Schofield five or six times since the beginning of August.
2. She says she is going to town to get a dress fitted but Norah Stoakes (friend of the agency) says she saw her coming out of Eden House Resort.
3. Aunt Mary acts as if she is up to something. She is dixtacted and sings to herself.

Norah smiled at "friend of the agency." "What does 'dixtacted' mean?" she asked them.

"You know—kind of absent-minded, as if she's always thinking of something else," said Gavin.

"Oh—*distracted*. You're right, she has been acting different. You've been very observant."

The Fearless Four beamed at her praise. "But now we're stuck," said Peter.

Ross, never able to sit still for long, climbed on a stool and began swinging from the top of the doorway. "We're stuck because we can't *trail* her," he said. "We aren't allowed to take the boat out alone until we're thirteen."

"So, Norah …" Ross dropped with a thud and all four looked at her expectantly.

"So you want *me* to take you in the boat and drop you off so you can follow her," said Norah. "But what if she sees you?"

"We'll be very, very careful," said Gavin. "We know how to track people quietly. We've been practising on the aunts—we followed them all the way to the gazebo and back without getting caught."

Norah reflected on how good she was at tracking Andrew. In spite of a reluctance to invade Aunt Mary's privacy, she felt a twinge of excitement, as if she were their age again. Maybe she could do more than just take them over in the boat. It would be almost a relief to have a holiday from her feelings for Andrew. She picked up a Captain Wonder comic from the floor and flipped through it while she decided.

"Okay," she said finally. She hushed their eager voices. "I think I'd better help you track her, though. You'll need someone to help make up an excuse if you're caught. And five of us will attract too much attention. I'll take Gavin and one other."

"Me! Me!"

"Sally," said Gavin at once. "She's the best at tracking." The other boys looked disappointed but accepted his decision. It had always surprised Norah how they let Gavin lead them, even though Peter was a year older. Somehow his gentle manner carried a lot of authority.

"I'll have to get permission," said Norah. "It'll be tricky because we won't know she's going until the last moment and she might take the *Putt-Putt*. And remember, Aunt Mary may not be up to *anything*—there could be some logical explanation." She knew from their eager faces that they didn't believe that, and all at once she didn't want to believe it either. "I'll be your Chief Detective," she continued. "You'll have to do exactly what I say." Then she added, a bit sheepishly, "Can I borrow a few of these comics?"

For the rest of that day they all observed Aunt Mary's movements. But she didn't appear on the dock in her hat until the next afternoon, when Mr. Hancock drove her away in the *Florence*. Gavin dashed up to tell Norah and Norah tried to appear nonchalant as she looked for an Elder. She found Aunt Anne in the kitchen, helping Hanny roll out piecrust.

"May I please take Gavin and Sally to Port Schofield in the *Putt-Putt*?" she asked.

As usual Aunt Anne looked uncertain. "Why do you want to go there?"

"To buy some comics and have ice cream."

"I wonder … I suppose it's all right. But make sure they wear life-jackets. How long are you going to be?"

"We'll be back by five," promised Norah. She skipped out before she could be questioned further.

Gavin and Sally looked solemn as they sat side by side in the bow of the *Putt-Putt*, muffled in fat orange life-jackets.

"I think we should moor at the hotel, not in town," said Norah. "After all, we're assuming that's where she is." She slowed down the boat and turned in to the hotel dock. A few guests sitting in wooden chairs along the shore glanced up at them. Not at all sure if they were allowed to use the dock, Norah tied up the painter quickly and hissed at the others. "Quick! Take off your life-jackets and follow me." The three detectives strolled across the lawn as if they were guests too. They hurried up the long path and retreated under a clump of trees for a conference.

"So far, so good," said Gavin, his eyes dancing. "Stop laughing, Sally!" He pulled out his notebook and began to scribble while Norah examined the hotel.

How were they ever going to find Aunt Mary? The huge three-storey building in front of them must contain hundreds of people.

"What are you writing, Gavin?" asked Sally.

"The colours of those chairs and where this hiding place is," he told her.

"That's not important," said Norah. "You don't have to write everything down, just what's relevant."

"But you never know what *could* be relevant," said Gavin, continuing to scribble.

Norah kept staring at the hotel, thinking hard. "Let's walk all the way around the outside," she suggested. "Maybe we'll spot her on the verandah. Now remember, look as if you're staying here. If she spots us we'll say ... Oh, yikes, what *will* we say?"

"We could say that we're visiting Mummy's friend," said Sally. "You know, Mrs. Abercrombie. She's staying here all month. She was on the island last week with her daughter. *Enid*," she added with disgust.

Norah looked at Sally with exasperation. "But why didn't you say so earlier? It's a perfect excuse. You could say I brought you over to play with Enid!"

"Ugh!" said Sally. "She's so babyish, isn't she, Gavin?" Gavin nodded.

"Still, that's our alibi—don't forget! Let's just hope we don't have to use it."

They began circling the lawn underneath the verandah, pulling their sun hats down over their faces. A group of well-dressed people were playing croquet. "There she is!" whispered Sally.

"Aunt Mary?" breathed Norah.

"No—Enid. And her mother." A small girl in a frilly dress was standing on the edge of the group, licking an ice cream cone while her mother bent over her and wiped her chin.

"Don't let them see us!" Norah grabbed each of them by the hand and headed back around the corner.

"I'm hungry!" complained Sally. "Couldn't we get some ice cream too?"

"Not yet," said Norah. She looked at her watch. "If we haven't found Aunt Mary by four-thirty we'll take the boat into town and get some."

They strolled back and forth aimlessly, avoiding the croquet game. Norah was just beginning to get up the courage to venture into the hotel itself when Gavin called *"Look!"*

"Shhh!" Norah pressed her hand over his mouth as a woman turned around at his voice. "Stay calm—sit down on the grass and don't turn your head. Did you really see her?"

Gavin nodded and leaned over to whisper into her ear. "She's out on the lake! In a boat! Left of the boathouse—I saw her yellow hat."

Carefully Norah raised her eyes. Sure enough, Aunt Mary was in the bow of a red canoe, her back to them. And someone was with her—a stocky man who steered awkwardly, making the canoe go in a wavering line.

"Good for you, Gavin! Okay, be as quiet as mice—we'll follow the canoe from the shore."

They ran lightly down to the lake and slunk along the shoreline behind the screen of trees. The canoe was far enough out that they wouldn't be seen. Soon it rounded a promontory ahead of them.

"Be *very* quiet," warned Norah. "We don't know how close it'll be to the shore on the other side." They got on their stomachs and slithered over the rocks until they could peek over.

The canoe had turned in to a tiny cove below them.

The man hauled it up on the beach, then held out his hand to Aunt Mary. They sat on some rocks, Aunt Mary drawing her legs up under her dress.

Before Norah could stop them, Gavin and Sally had crept through the bushes to get closer. She joined them reluctantly. Suddenly it felt wrong to spy on Aunt Mary like this. Whoever this man was, it wasn't their business. She imagined her guardian's hurt face if she caught them.

"Let's go," she whispered to the others when she reached them. "We've seen enough."

"Not yet," entreated Gavin, digging out his notebook. "I need to describe him."

Norah fidgeted while he looked and scribbled. Aunt Mary and the stranger were talking intently to each other, their voices too far away to be heard. But Aunt Mary's frequent laughter floated up to them. The man looked as old as she was; he took off his hat and his white hair caught the light. At least they were both facing the lake, not the trees.

After what seemed like an eternity, the couple got into the canoe again and the three detectives trailed them back to the hotel dock. They hid behind the boathouse as the canoe arrived. Now they could hear every word.

"Just look at the time! I must get back to town before Mr. Hancock comes. Goodbye, Tom. I've had a lovely afternoon."

"Goodbye, then, Mary. I'll see you on Friday at three." The man lifted his hat as Aunt Mary hurried past the boathouse.

"Who *is* he?" whispered Sally.

"Not yet!" hissed Norah. "No talking until we get out of here. Wait until he's gone too." The man finished tying up the canoe and went up the path. When he reached the hotel, they got into their own boat.

Gavin whipped out his notebook, but Norah clapped her hand over his. "Don't write anything!" she ordered. "As soon as we get back to Gairloch we'll have a meeting."

"But aren't we going to have any ice cream?" asked Sally.

"No!" said Norah fiercely. "We're going straight back before Mr. Hancock comes. But you can say you had ice cream if your mother asks you what you did."

"That's not fair—" began Sally, but the engine revved and Norah drove back to the island as fast as she could.

"THIS CASE didn't turn out to be very interesting," said Gavin, back in the playhouse. An indignant Peter and Ross had been shooed out of it. "All she does is visit that man. But wasn't it exciting when we were following the canoe?"

"Is he her *boy friend*?" giggled Sally. "Aunt Mary's too old to have a boy friend!"

Norah's thoughts raced. "Of course she is," she agreed. "He's probably just a friend of the family."

"So why does she keep it a secret?" persisted Sally.

"Uhh ... maybe he's someone Aunt Florence doesn't like. You know how many people she disapproves of."

"Like Bernard," said Gavin. "Bernard is our friend in Toronto," he explained to Sally. "When Norah first knew him she had to meet him secretly—even I didn't know. She doesn't have to do that any more, but Aunt Florence still doesn't like him much. She's always telling me how 'unsuitable' Bernard is because his mother's a cleaning woman."

"And if you'd *known* that I was meeting him, you wouldn't have told Aunt Florence, would you?" Norah asked him.

"Of course not!"

"Well, this is the same situation. Aunt Mary obviously wants to keep her visits a secret—but now *we* know. So we have to keep it a secret too. Do you understand? We can't tell anyone, or we'll get her into trouble with Aunt Florence. I don't even want you to write it down in your casebook, Gavin."

"But—" Gavin looked deflated, but then he sighed and said, "Okay, Norah, I won't."

"But can't we tell Peter and Ross?" asked Sally. "They're waiting to hear what happened!"

Norah knew they'd tell them anyway. "All right ... but no one else! You've solved the case and you did it very well, but we found out something we shouldn't have known—and we don't want to hurt Aunt Mary, right?"

They nodded solemnly. Norah made them each say cross-my-heart-and-hope-to-die. Then she left them and climbed up to her rock.

She stretched out on her stomach, trying to absorb all they'd seen. Aunt Mary's secret was probably safe. To the Fearless Four, everyone except herself was an Elder and therefore not to be trusted.

But what did the secret mean? Of course the man *was* Aunt Mary's "boy friend." Norah had known that at once from the tender way they had looked at each other. Now she recognized in Aunt Mary the same symptoms she possessed herself.

Most important of all—his name was Tom! That meant he was *Thomas,* Aunt Mary's long-ago love, who had somehow come back into her life. He must be visiting from the prairies, just so he could see Aunt Mary.

No wonder she'd wanted to talk about Thomas with Norah that night! It was the same reason that Norah was always trying to casually introduce Andrew's name into conversations. Norah wished Aunt Mary had told her she was seeing him again, but she was probably afraid to reveal that even to Norah.

She glanced at Aunt Mary all evening and pressed up against her when Aunt Florence was reading. Aunt Mary smiled and squeezed her shoulder.

Surely she would soon have the courage to tell her mother—and this time she wouldn't give in. Then she would marry Tom and live happily ever after—just like all the songs and movies.

Norah's own love was far more insecure, especially since so much of it had to wait until she was older. She gazed at Andrew, who looked lost in a daydream as he stared at the fire. It was wonderful that she could talk to him again, but even that was no longer enough. He thought of her the same way he thought of Janet or Flo.

She knew what she had to do. She had to *tell* him, to reveal her feelings. Then he would realize that he loved her too and he would wait for her until she was old enough to marry him.

None of the songs or movies said how loving someone required all these difficult tasks.

9

Stormy Weather

*N*orah and Janet sat together on the dock, listening to Clare's mother rant at her. Her furious voice drifted out of the open window of the Girls' Dorm. She had appeared there after breakfast and grimly ordered everyone out so she and Clare could have a "talk."

"You are completely irresponsible, Clare! How could you possibly forget them?"

"I just did," said Clare sullenly. "I didn't want to take them anyway—they talked me into it. They should have noticed when I was leaving."

Yesterday Clare had taken her brothers with her when she drove the *Putt-Putt* to visit her friend Louise on Cliff Island. The little boys had gone off to play on the rocks and Clare, forgetting all about them, had returned alone. Louise's father had had to bring back Peter and Ross, tearful and scared; Ross had scraped his knee badly.

Clare's mother, who'd been visiting some friends on one of the other lakes for a few days, had arrived back very late herself and only heard about the mishap this morning.

Norah and Janet glanced at each other uneasily as Aunt Mar's voice grew more shrill. They shouldn't be eavesdropping, but they couldn't resist hearing Clare get into trouble.

"Clare Drummond, you are fifteen years old, not a child! If your father was here he'd be very disappointed in you. Why can't you be more like Norah? She takes such good care of Gavin."

"Oh, *Norah*," said Clare scornfully. "I'm sick of hearing about perfect Norah. Just because she's a war guest she gets treated differently. Not like me. This family is so mean to me...," she howled.

Janet rolled her eyes. "What a baby," she whispered. "Don't worry, Norah, she didn't mean it."

Norah knew she did, but she tried to tell herself she didn't care.

"You're grounded for a week," Aunt Mar was saying. "That means not leaving the island at all—not by yourself or with anyone else."

"That's not *fair*! I didn't mean to leave them, I just forgot!" But her mother was already gone, not even noticing Norah and Janet as she marched past them up the steps.

"Well, I'm not going to stay out here all morning," said Janet. "I was in the middle of painting my toenails."

They ventured into the boathouse again, pretending to ignore Clare, crumpled up on her bed and sobbing into her pillow. "Everyone picks on me," she wailed. "It's not *fair* ..."

Janet put on "In the Blue of the Evening" and hummed along.

"Turn that off! I don't feel like listening to records!" Clare hurled her pillow towards Janet and it landed on the record, sending the needle screeching across it.

"*Now* look what you've done! You've ruined it!" Janet snatched up the record, examined the ugly scratch, then threw it down and dashed out the door.

"That was really mean," said Norah. "It was her favourite."

"Oh you shut up! It's none of your business, Norah Stoakes—you're not part of this family. You should be grateful that we took you in. And another thing, Norah— I've noticed how you follow Andrew around. You may as well give up. You're not nearly good enough for him. Anyway, you're only thirteen—it looks ridiculous for someone your age to go mooning after a nineteen-year-old."

Norah was speechless. She almost jumped on Clare and pulled her hair. Last summer she would have. But now she just wanted to get away from her.

"You—you are *despicable*!" she hissed. She ran out even faster than Janet had and didn't stop until she collapsed on her rock.

Clare knew about Andrew! Would she tell Janet and Flo? Worse, would she tell Andrew? Did *everyone* know? Were they all laughing at her?

Norah sat up and hugged her knees against her sweaty blouse. If only it were last summer, when her life at Gairloch was so simple. She almost wished she could cast off her feelings for Andrew. But she couldn't—it was as if she had an incurable disease.

And she hardly even saw Andrew these days, which made her long for him all the more. He'd been spending all his time with a family on the mainland. Janet told her they were the brothers and sister of a boy he'd been very close to who was now in the air force. Jamie and Lois and Dick Mitchell, his friends were called. Norah smouldered with jealousy every time she heard their names.

Two hours later Norah sat listlessly on the dock with her fishing rod. She'd had a long swim but she was already hot again. Thunder rumbled in the distance; a storm was holding its breath but couldn't let it out.

"Any luck, Norah?" Aunt Catherine stood behind her, holding her knitting and fanning her face with her hand. "I thought I'd come down and sit by the water to see if I could catch a breeze. I certainly wish the weather would break. Just listen to those cicadas buzz! They're always especially loud before a storm."

Norah didn't tell her that her hook wasn't even baited. She tried to smile at Aunt Catherine but could only manage a shrug.

Aunt Catherine pulled one of the heavy wooden chairs up beside her. "You look rather seedy, Norah. I hope you're not coming down with anything. Do you feel all right?"

"Mmmm," said Norah, trying to control her irritation. It wasn't like Aunt Catherine to be this nosy.

"Everyone seems to be under the weather today," continued the old lady. "'Under the weather'—that's a very appropriate phrase when you think of it, as if the weather held us all squirming under its thumb. Mar is upset with Clare—and I must say, that child gets more impossible all the time. Dorothy told Mar that she shouldn't have been away so long—now Mar isn't speaking to her. Florence and Bea are having the most absurd argument over how to pronounce 'forsythia.' And Mary seems to be off on a cloud. She forgot it was her turn to help with the children's breakfast, which is quite uncharacteristic. What a family ... Sometimes I'm glad I'm not really part of it. Aren't you?"

Norah nodded. At least Aunt Catherine was once again confiding in her like an equal.

"I don't think Andrew's been very happy lately either," mused Aunt Catherine. "Poor lad. I'm so very fond of him and I can't abide the idea of him going off to this monstrous war."

Norah's skin prickled with alertness. "But that won't be for a few years, not until he finishes university," she said. "Maybe the war will be over by then."

"Let's hope so. If it isn't, he's going to be doing something that's against his nature—I feel sorry for boys like him."

"What do you mean?"

"I mean he's not cut out to be a soldier. They all want him to be like the other men in the family—like Hugh. Now Hugh was a dear, but he was a completely different sort from Andrew."

Norah was puzzled. "But he *must* want to be a soldier. He *should* join the war." She shuddered. "Not until he has to, of course."

"Should he?" Aunt Catherine's lined face looked tired. "I lost a father, a brother and a nephew—Hugh—in wars, Norah. It's a wicked waste."

"But we have to beat Hitler!"

"I don't know how to answer that, Norah. Yes, we have to beat him. But what a price we're paying! Not just our side—think of what the German people are enduring. We're bombing them just as heavily as they've been bombing Britain." She broke off a piece of wool angrily. "It's all so *senseless*! Do you know what we called the *last* war? 'The war to end all wars.' *Huh!*"

Then she sighed. "Poor Andrew. He was born at the wrong time. Let's just hope your little brother will be luckier."

Norah couldn't bear to think of Gavin fighting in a war. But if he did, he'd be doing it because he had no choice. Like Andrew. Surely Aunt Catherine was wrong. Andrew *must* want to fight Hitler. If he didn't, he'd be a coward—wouldn't he?

"I shouldn't burden you with all these sombre thoughts, Norah. Are you sure there's nothing troubling you?" Aunt Catherine peered at her and Norah looked away. "Lately you haven't seemed yourself."

"I'm all right," mumbled Norah. It was tempting to tell Aunt Catherine about her feelings for Andrew, but after all she *was* an Elder. And she wouldn't understand, anyway. She'd never married and she'd probably never even been in love.

"Ah, well," said Aunt Catherine, pulling out her knitting. "It's just being thirteen. *I'd* never want to be thirteen again—a miserable, muddled age."

Surprisingly, this cheered Norah. She wouldn't always *be* thirteen, she thought suddenly—there was a light at the end of the tunnel. One day she'd be eighty-three and looking back on herself as calmly as Aunt Catherine was doing. But the thought of being as old as Aunt Catherine was too slippery to hang on to.

THAT EVENING the air outside still crackled with impending fury. Inside, the atmosphere was the same: a cloud of discord hung over the family.

During the children's dinner, Norah sat as far away from Clare as she could and tried not to look at her. Janet, on the other hand, glared at her cousin all through the meal. Clare made spiteful comments to her brothers for getting her into trouble. After both meals were over, the family sat woodenly in the living room, someone occasionally making a stiff remark about the weather.

Aunt Mar and Aunt Dorothy were glaring at each other as much as their daughters. "Why aren't you girls doing your knitting?" complained Aunt Dorothy, holding up a long grey sock to measure it. "I thought you were each going to make a scarf for a soldier this summer. Don't forget, not everyone leads the comfortable life you do. There's a war on, you know."

"There's a war on, moron," whispered Clare.

"Don't you be rude to my mother!" Janet hissed back.

Aunt Catherine suggested a game of rummy and four of the Elders gathered around a table. For a while the only sound was the ripple and snap of cards being shuffled.

"A run of five!" gloated Uncle Reg. "Your turn, Florence."

"For*sigh*thia," said Aunt Florence quietly.

"For*sith*ia!" retorted her sister.

"It was named after a Mr. Forsythe—therefore it is pronounced the same way as his name," sniffed Aunt Florence.

Aunt Bea didn't even look up from her cards as she muttered, "Madge Allwood, who was the best gardener in Montreal, *always* said 'Forsithia.'"

"Really, Bea." Aunt Florence threw down her cards in disgust. "If you won't see reason I refuse to go on playing."

"Now what on earth does how a flower's name is pronounced have to do with a game of cards?" Uncle Reg asked.

Aunt Florence bridled. "It's not a flower, it's a shrub. And what do *you* know about gardening, Reg? It's not your quarrel—kindly stay out of it."

"I don't see why there has to be a quarrel at all," said Andrew quietly, looking up from his book.

Norah, hiding behind *her* book, was surprised to see the aunts look ashamed.

"You're perfectly right, Andrew," said Aunt Florence briskly. "Let's talk about *you*." She gazed at him fondly.

"It's going to be such a treat to have you in Toronto this year. I do wish you'd live with us, but I know you boys need your freedom. What are you taking in first term?"

As Andrew recited the names of his engineering courses Norah wriggled with excitement. She had forgotten that Andrew would be living in the same city. Surely he'd come over for meals.

"Hugh would have liked to take engineering," sighed Aunt Florence. "You are so much like him, my dear. My poor Hugh …"

Aunt Bea cut in abruptly. "How's your friend Jack doing, Andrew? What mischief you two boys both got up to! You used to spend the whole summer pretending you were savages and smearing yourselves with paint— without any clothes on, if I remember!" She giggled. "Do you hear from him much?"

"I've had a few letters," said Andrew guardedly. "And of course the Mitchells hear from him. He's all right—he hasn't seen much action yet."

"It must make you want to be in on it, when your best friend is," said Uncle Barclay. "Too bad he's older than you—you could have joined up together."

"But Andrew is going to join the army, not the air force," said Aunt Florence proudly. "All the Drummonds and Ogilvies have been army men. You're going to try to get into Hugh's old regiment, aren't you, dear? He would have been so proud of you."

"Florence!" Everyone froze at the hysterical edge in Aunt Bea's voice. "I've always wanted to say this and now

I'm going to. You dwell too much on that sainted son of yours. He's gone—why can't you accept it? No one ever talks about *my* son, and he's alive and prospering. I am tired of always hearing about perfect Hugh, and I'm sure Andrew is as well."

In the shocked silence the thunder rolled more ominously. Gerald ducked his head at his mother's words. Aunt Florence drew herself upright, took a deep breath and began to explode just as the storm did.

"How *dare* you ..." she began.

CRA-AAA-CK! Sally screamed and ran to her mother as the thunder crashed and the clouds emptied onto the roof with a deafening rattle.

Aunt Anne hustled out all the younger children. The older cousins exchanged looks and fled as well. They huddled on the verandah and watched the teeming rain, listening to Aunt Florence's rage compete with the storm. Aunt Bea, Uncle Reg and Aunt Mar's voices soon joined the fray.

"What's *wrong* with this family?" Flo's face was angry and pale. "They're so petty! Don't they realize there are more important things to worry about?"

"I wish they'd stop," said Janet, close to tears. "I hate it when they go on like this."

Flo put her arm around her sister. "Let's just forget about them. *We'll* never be like that. Come on—we'll run to the boathouse and I'll teach you all how to play bridge. Do you want to come, Andrew?"

Andrew had been staring into the storm silently, the

flashes of lightning illuminating his twitching face.
"Thanks, Flo, but I think I'll have an early night." He ran
off into the rain.

"Coming, Norah?" The prospect of getting soaked
made Janet giggle.

"I think I'll just stay on the verandah for a while." She
watched the others dash shrieking down the steps.

Norah went along the verandah to the side door. She
slipped into the hall off the kitchen and found what she
was looking for—a long rubber raincoat. While she was
slithering into it she spied Hanny washing the dishes with
a grim look on her face. Her husband sat at the table,
pulling on his pipe. They must be able to hear everything
that was being shouted in the living room.

The coat came down to her feet and its sleeves flopped
below her hands, but at least it would keep her dry. Pulling
the hood over her head, she ventured into the storm.

The rain streamed off her as she groped her way down
the hill to Andrew's cabin. The clammy coat made her
perspire, but her bare feet were cold against the wet rocks.

Norah circled the cabin restlessly, longing to knock on
Andrew's door and have another talk. Then she could *tell*
him. But she didn't have the nerve. The hood of the coat
blocked her vision; she flung it back and let the driving
rain sluice over her head. Leaning against the wall underneath Andrew's window, she tipped back her head and
caught the heavy drops in her mouth.

Finally the rain settled into a steady shower and the
thunder and lightening grew fainter. Then Norah heard

another sound. The sound of someone crying—crying with such desperate gulps that Norah trembled.

It was Andrew—who else could it be? Through his open window she listened to his wrenching sobs, his deep voice gasping for air.

The only time Norah had seen a man cry was when her father had said goodbye to her and Gavin in England. That had been a few controlled tears. This was as violent as the storm had been.

She took a chance and heaved herself up by the windowsill to look into the room. Her aching arms would just let her up for a second. It was long enough to glimpse Andrew sprawled on the couch, his head in his arms and his shoulders shuddering.

Norah slid out of the heavy coat, rolled it up into a ball under her arm and sped away into the night. When she reached the dock she peeled off the rest of her wet clothes and jumped into the lake. The water tingled against her bare skin and her body felt as liquid as the lake and the rain.

Janet poked out her head. "Norah's skinny-dipping!"

In an instant she and Flo and Clare had joined her in the black lake. They whooped and splashed and Norah tried to drown the shock of Andrew's misery.

10

A Visitor

All the next day the cleansing rain fell on the island. When Norah went up to breakfast, Aunt Dorothy and Aunt Mar were setting the children's table together, singing "Pack Up Your Troubles" and tittering like girls. The rest of the Elders, looking as shamefaced as children who had misbehaved, pussyfooted around each other with careful politeness.

"Aunt Florence told me never to mention that shrub word again," said Gavin solemnly, as he joined Norah on the verandah. "She says when we get back to the city she'll check with the university and then she'll know she's right—but she wants the arguing to stop."

Norah shrugged as she swung in the glider.

"Are you in a bad mood?" Gavin asked her. Bosley galloped up the stairs and shook a fountain over both of them.

She shrugged again, but because it was Gavin, managed a small smile.

"Would you like to have Creature for a while?" Gavin pulled the small stuffed elephant out of his raincoat pocket and handed him over.

Norah took Creature gingerly. His wool body was grimy and one ear was missing. He stank.

"Thanks, Gavin. Why does he smell so awful?"

"He got into the fish guts when we were cleaning some bass."

"Pee-yew! Why don't you wash him?"

"No!" said Gavin with alarm. "Haney says that too, but he might come apart—he almost did the last time he had a bath. You can keep him until tonight. I have to go now, we're having an important meeting. Come on, Boz!" He and the dog ran off to join the other members of the Fearless Four.

Norah set Creature on the verandah railing to air out. Everyone but her was feeling better. But what about Andrew? He hadn't appeared yet, and she was too tired to go check on him. Tired and sluggish, as if she'd been awake all night, even though she'd fallen asleep instantly after their swim. And her stomach felt bloated. Maybe she should go in and ask Hanny for some Castoria, but the thought of that disgusting liquid made her want to gag.

Why had Andrew been crying? Norah swung her chair violently. Was it because the family had been comparing him to Hugh? But he must be used to that. It could have been because of what he had told her—that he would rather be an actor than an engineer. She clenched her fists—they should let him do what he wanted.

Or perhaps he was crying because he didn't want to be in the war. Maybe Aunt Catherine was right and Andrew didn't want to fight. Maybe he *was* afraid.

Norah herself was frightened of the war. Every so often she had a terrible nightmare that her family's house was being bombed to rubble. In the daytime it was easy to reassure herself. She and Gavin had been evacuated overseas to get away from bombs and the threat of an invasion, but now both dangers were more remote. She knew from school and the news that Hitler no longer threatened to invade Britain, and the terrible bombing it had received when she'd first lived in Canada had let up considerably. But her night-time self didn't seem to have absorbed that yet.

Andrew, however, was not supposed to be afraid—he was perfect! If he no longer fit into the neat category of a hero, she would have to alter her fantasies. Now there seemed to be parts of him she didn't know at all.

She still loved him. If only she had the courage to tell him, it would help him be brave, the way Flo's letters to her boy friends did.

Andrew Drummond, the youngest ever recipient of the Victoria Cross, said in a recent interview that he got over his initial fear of fighting through the inspiration of his beloved fiancée, Norah.

But today her fantasies couldn't console her. She curled up on the seat of the glider and listened to the rain increase its drumming. Janet and Clare were playing ping-pong on the table at the far end of the verandah. The monotonous click of the ball, and their giggles when one of them missed, made Norah scowl. How could Janet forgive Clare so easily? But the two of them were cousins; that gave them a bond Norah would never have.

"And what is young Norah doing out here all by herself? I've just made a fire in the living room—wouldn't you be warmer in there?" Hanny's placid, plump husband stood beside her, his clothes covered with pieces of bark.

"I like it better here," said Norah, sitting up again. "Thanks anyway."

"You're a funny one," smiled Mr. Hancock. "Suit yourself." He ambled around the corner and Norah resumed her curled-up position. She could hear talking in the living room; Uncle Reg and Uncle Barclay were playing checkers.

Usually she liked lazy wet days at Gairloch. She could go in and work on the puzzle; she'd never managed to finish it in one summer. But she felt trapped in a sticky web of inertia. She stayed half-asleep in her chair for an hour, until her cramping stomach forced her inside to the bathroom.

FIFTEEN MINUTES LATER, Norah lay on a folded towel on her bed, shaking so much that her teeth clacked. She pulled her blanket tighter around her shoulders.

Something was wrong with her! Somehow she had injured herself inside—or she was terribly sick.

She had to tell someone, and soon. But who? There were too many possible people: Aunt Mary, Aunt Florence, Aunt Catherine or Hanny. They would all be kind and concerned. But it would be so embarrassing to say *where* she was hurt. And how could she make it up to the cottage?

There was only one person she wanted. *"Mum ... "* whispered Norah, sitting up and rocking back and forth. "Oh, Mum ..."

"Norah!" Flo was shaking her shoulder. "Norah, what on earth is the matter? You look terrified!"

"I want my *m-mother,*" croaked Norah. "I *need* her, and she's so far away ..."

Flo sat on the bed and hugged Norah. "You poor thing. But why are you so homesick all of a sudden? What's happened?"

"Oh, Flo ..." Norah looked up at the older girl desperately. "Something's wrong with me! I'm *bleeding ...*"

Slowly she choked out where. To her astonishment Flo began to smile.

"Norah, it's all right! It's perfectly natural, what's happened to you. Didn't you know? Hasn't Aunt Florence told you?"

"Told me what?" Relief flooded through Norah at Flo's matter-of-factness. At least she wasn't going to die. But what was she talking about?

"I guess I'll have to tell you then. Listen, Norah." The older girl flushed. "You know that babies grow inside a woman's stomach, don't you?"

Norah nodded, a dim memory in her head of her mother, huge with Gavin, leaning over her in the tub and telling her she had a baby inside her.

"Well, when you start to grow up you make a kind of lining inside yourself for the baby to live in."

"What baby?" This was getting more confusing every moment.

"No baby yet. But your body doesn't know it's not time for one. So the lining comes—well, it comes out—and it's made of tissues and stuff that looks like blood. It lasts a few days, then it stops. Oh dear. I don't think I'm explaining this very well. I wish I could remember what Mother said when she told me—it made sense then."

Light dawned. "You mean—the visitor? The little man who sweeps you out?"

"*What?*"

Shyly Norah told Flo what Aunt Florence had said.

"No wonder you didn't understand! What a stupid way to tell you. That must be why some women call it their 'little visitor.' I call it 'the curse.'"

"The curse! That sounds horrible!"

Flo shrugged. "It does, I guess. I never really thought about it, it's just what my friends and I say. I guess because it's such a nuisance, putting up with it every month. But you get used to it."

Norah was still digesting her earlier words—that this was normal and would only last a few days. Would she have to stay in bed all that time? she wondered.

Then she realized what Flo had just said. "What do you mean, once a month?" she asked suspiciously. "This isn't going to keep on happening, is it?"

Flo looked apologetic. "Uhhh, yes, I'm afraid so, Norah. Once every month until you're about fifty. Then you stop. And you don't do it if you're pregnant, of course."

Norah looked at her with horror. "Once a month until I'm fifty! That's forever!" She sat up straighter, pushed back her hair and said haughtily, "I'm not going to have anything to do with this curse! I won't *do* it!"

Flo laughed so hard she wiped tears from her face. "Norah, you are so funny! You *have* to do it—you don't have a choice. It just—it just happens."

Norah was filled with an enormous lassitude. Something inside her said that Flo was right; mysterious ads in magazines and whispered remarks at school suddenly made sense. She listened dully while the other girl, embarrassed again, started mumbling about sanitary belts and something called Kotex. In the middle of it Janet burst in.

"What's up?"

"Oh, nothing drastic ..." said Flo. "Norah just got the curse and I'm telling her about it."

"Lucky you!" said Janet passionately. She gazed at Norah with clear admiration. "I wish *I* would start. I'm so slow. Mother says she didn't get it until she was fifteen—she thinks you start younger in each generation. But now I'm *fourteen* ..."

"Why would you ever want to?" asked Norah with astonishment.

"Because then I'll be a grown-up. Because getting the curse means you're a woman and can have babies—when you're older, of course, and when ... well ..." She blushed, and so did Norah.

"Did you two *know* about babies?" said Flo. "If there's something you don't understand, you can ask me." She looked important and they both realized that she knew things that they didn't.

"No thanks," said Janet stiffly. "I'll ask *Mother* if I want to find out anything."

Flo lost her secretive look. "That's probably the best. And Norah can ask her mother when she gets back to England."

Norah thought she knew what Flo was hinting at, but she was quite willing to let the details wait until she was older.

It was bad enough having to deal with this ... this *curse*. Although Janet's envy made her feel rather proud. She, a year younger, had begun first!

"Has Clare started?" she asked them.

"Clare started at twelve," said Flo. "That's why it makes me mad that no one told you properly—you could have been even earlier!"

Norah sighed and looked at Flo helplessly. "Umm— I need to get some of that Kotex soon, Flo."

"Of course you do—but I don't think I'm the one who should help you. I'll get one of the aunts. Who do you want?"

At first Norah started to say Aunt Mary, but she knew how embarrassed she would be. Aunt Florence would be calm and efficient, and besides, she was the one who'd brought it up in the first place.

"Aunt Florence, I guess." Flo ran up to the cottage.

"Why didn't you *tell* me?" Norah asked Janet. "If you knew all along, you could have said something."

Janet's fat cheeks turned pink. "I'm sorry ... I guess I thought you knew. I thought everyone our age knew. Anyway, your mother tells you. Oh, Norah, I'm sorry! I mean, I thought Aunt Florence would have told you."

"She tried," said Norah wearily.

Aunt Florence marched up the boathouse stairs, a package under her arm. "Out you go, Janet. Now, Norah, I have exactly what you need. Aren't you glad I informed you just in time? There's nothing to worry about, it's all perfectly natural ..." Her briskness put the whole traumatic morning into perspective. Norah sighed and submitted herself to this new feminine ritual.

"You won't tell anyone but Aunt Mary, will you?" Norah had a vision of Aunt Florence announcing it at dinner to the whole clan.

"Of course not—it's not something you talk about." Her guardian gave her an odd, sad look. "Hmm ... when we get back to Toronto, Norah, I'm going to take you shopping for a brassiere." She kissed the top of Norah's head. "You're growing up, my dear. I don't know if I like that or not."

11

A Trip to Town

$\mathcal{F}$ or the next day or so, Norah spent so much time reading in her glider that she felt as if she were planted there. To her relief no one seemed to notice she was any different, and when Aunt Florence and Flo and Janet gave her special smiles she was comforted.

"You don't need to rest all the time," Aunt Florence told her. "You're not ill."

But although Norah felt perfectly all right, the shock of what had happened to her made her want to pretend to be an invalid. And, anyway, she couldn't go swimming—that was the worst part.

"What are you up to, Norah?" Andrew's voice startled her from her book. She'd finally borrowed *Wuthering Heights* and was immersed in the turbulent saga of Catherine and Heathcliff.

She shrugged and smiled shyly. "Did you have a good time?" She knew he'd been on a canoe trip with the Mitchells.

"Wonderful! We almost dumped all our food overboard, though." He was so cheerful that his wretched sobbing seemed like something she had dreamt.

"I need to go to Brockhurst," Andrew continued. "Hanny asked me to pick up her cooking pot—it's having a hole mended. Mr. Hancock has taken all the aunts to see the gardens at Beaumaris and everyone else seems to have disappeared this afternoon. Do you want to come?"

"Oh, yes please!" Trying to control the excitement in her voice, Norah added, "Do you think I need to tell someone?"

"You can tell Hanny. Why don't you meet me on the dock in ten minutes?"

Norah forgot about being an invalid. She ran into the kitchen to tell Hanny, then raced down to the Girls' Dorm with all the energy of her former self. The others had rowed over to Little Island for a picnic. Thank goodness none of them was here to see her leave alone with Andrew—especially Clare.

A few minutes later Norah sat in the *Putt-Putt* opposite Andrew, gloating over her good fortune. Not only did she have him to herself for the rest of the afternoon, she hadn't been to Brockhurst yet this year. She had changed into a skirt and borrowed, without asking, Clare's straw hat. In her lap she held a purse Flo had given her. Since she was now officially a teen-ager, she might as well act the part.

To her surprise, Andrew headed towards Ford's Bay and moored the boat there.

"Aren't we going by water?" asked Norah.

"Aunt Florence told me this morning that I could take her car."

"Do you know how to *drive*?" blurted out Norah, then flushed when Andrew laughed.

"Don't worry—I'm an expert. Climb in, Miss Stoakes, and I'll show you."

Norah started to rush into the car, then restrained herself and drew up each leg gracefully after she sat down. Just last week Clare had read aloud an article about how to get in and out of a car in a ladylike manner.

She leaned back and let the breeze ruffle her hair as Andrew sped up the dusty road. Tongue-tied with the bliss of sitting next to him, Norah gazed out the window as they passed through Glen Orchard and Bala, catching glimpses of the blue water through the firs. Andrew, as silent as her, concentrated on driving.

At last they arrived in Brockhurst. Andrew parked carefully at the edge of town and they headed towards the hardware store where the pot was being soldered. The man looked surprised to see them.

"Haven't had a chance to do it yet," he muttered. "You'd be best to come back tomorrow."

"I'm afraid we can't," said Andrew politely. "We don't mind waiting—could you have it done by four?" Grudgingly, the man agreed.

"Let's look around," suggested Andrew. "Then I'll buy you a milkshake."

Norah hung her purse over her arm and adjusted her hat, trying to look as if she were Andrew's girl friend. Brockhurst was crowded with tourists who had come up by train from Toronto. Norah and Andrew joined them, meandering in and out of stores and admiring the stately Opera House. They wandered down to the wharf and watched all the boats arriving and departing in the bay.

"Ready for a cold drink?" Andrew asked finally. "It's getting awfully hot."

"Yes, please," said Norah. She wanted to impress him with her brilliant conversation, but she could hardly manage those two words.

As they turned up Beach Road they saw a group of soldiers marching towards them, and stood on the side to let them pass: a long column of men with closely cropped hair, wearing uniforms that looked like pyjamas. Some of them carried shovels or rakes and one had a football under his arm.

"Who are they?" whispered Norah.

Andrew was staring at the men intently. "They're German prisoners of war," he whispered back.

"You mean—they're *Nazis*?"

"That's right. In fact, the Brockhurst camp is full of top-ranking ones."

Now Norah stared even harder, her legs trembling. Nazis in Canada? The men held up their heads proudly as they passed. Norah stepped closer to Andrew.

She simply couldn't believe it. They looked like any other men, not like monsters or villains—like the Enemy.

"Strange, isn't it?" said Andrew as the last of the men passed and .they continued back into town. "I've seen them before. They mark off an area in the bay with barbed wire where they swim." The muscle twitched in his cheek. "That's who I'll be fighting one day, Norah. They seem so ordinary, don't they?"

"But they must have done terrible things," said Norah in a small voice.

"No doubt they have." Andrew sighed, then picked up a rock and heaved it into the bushes. "But let's not worry about that on such a gorgeous day. Weren't we thinking about milkshakes? And look who's coming!"

Heading towards them were three teen-agers: a very pretty girl about Andrew's age and two younger boys. They were laughing loudly and shoving each other.

"Look who's here—it's the Great Andrew of Drummond!" cried one of the boys.

"Hello there, Mitchells! Norah, these are my crazy friends—Lois and Jamie and Dick Mitchell. This is Norah, my aunt's war guest. I don't know if I should be introducing you to these nutcases, Norah. I'm sure they're a bad influence. Would you all care to join us for a milkshake?" The four of them were obviously good friends. They continued to tease and fool around as they walked back into town.

Norah lagged a little behind, furious that her time alone with Andrew had ended. When they got to the ice cream store and scrambled into a booth, she sat at one end and eyed the newcomers warily. The two dark-haired boys looked so much alike they might have been twins, except one was shorter than the other. Lois was also dark, with glittering green eyes. Everything about her was smooth: her perfectly waved hair, her creamy white skin and her even features. Her voice had an ironic tone.

Norah tried to stay calm as Lois gave her a cool, appraising look. "That's a pretty purse you have, Norah," said Lois, as if Norah were a little girl pretending to be a grown-up. Sucking her milkshake hard, Norah glared at the other girl over the top of the container. She noticed how Lois continually drew Andrew's attention towards herself by touching his arm lightly or mocking him.

To her great relief the Mitchells left to meet their father. Now she had Andrew to herself again, but he still seemed to be with them in spirit. "What clowns," he laughed. "The whole family's like that—they're much less formal than *our* family. Everyone does what he wants and their grandmother is a scream. When Jack and I were little, she used to tell us wonderful stories about growing up in New York."

"Is Jack your best friend?" said Norah abruptly.

"I guess he is, although we've lived in different places for quite a while and we've—well, never mind. He's a marvellous fellow—the most intelligent person I know. One day he'll be a famous author. He already writes brilliant short stories and he's going to write about his war experiences—that will be something. He's the only friend I have who also wants to do something creative with his life. The difference is that *his* family is all for it," he added, his voice turning hard.

Norah was even jealous of Jack, and he was far away fighting. All at once she felt tired and stale. The milkshake had made her more thirsty, not less, and her sandalled feet were clogged with dust. She had been with Andrew an entire afternoon but hadn't managed to say anything to bring them closer.

"Let's go and see if that pot is ready," said Andrew. A few minutes later they were lugging the heavy iron pot towards the car. Then Andrew drove fast out of town.

"Do you want to try?" he asked, slowing down.

"What do you mean?"

"Do you want to try driving? It's perfectly safe—this part of the road is always deserted and I'll take the wheel if you get into trouble. My father used to sometimes let me drive when I was your age—along this very road."

Norah was so overcome she could only nod with shining eyes. Andrew pulled over and changed places with her. Patiently he explained the functions of the pedals and gearshift. Her heart thudded as she turned the key and the engine responded. Slowly she let out the clutch as he told her, and pressed the gas pedal gingerly. The car jerked a bit and then, like an obedient animal, rumbled along the road. She managed to shift into second and third without stalling.

Norah clenched the steering wheel so hard her knuckles stuck out sharply. "You can go a *little* faster," Andrew chuckled. "At this rate we won't be home until dark!"

"But what if someone comes?" asked Norah, staring pop-eyed ahead of her.

"Just keep to your side of the road and you'll be fine."

Luckily no one did come. After a few minutes Norah relaxed a bit and began to enjoy driving. She liked the feeling of the car's power under her control and went a little faster, giggling when the car responded as if it had wanted to speed up.

"I'd better take over now," said Andrew. "We're coming to a crossroad. You did very well," he added, as Norah geared down, turned into the side of the road and stopped.

"Thank you," she breathed. "That was super! When I grow up I'd like to be a chauffeur or something. But Clare says I can't."

"Why not?"

"She says only men can be chauffeurs."

"Don't listen to Clare," said Andrew, sliding into the driver's seat. "Women can do a lot more things than they used to. My mother drives a huge ambulance in Winnipeg. She loves it! Be a chauffeur, if that's what you want. Don't let anyone stop you—okay?"

"Okay," said Norah, too overcome to suggest that he should do what *he* wanted to as well. She sat beside him in a dream the rest of the way to Ford's Bay. She'd driven a car! Even her mother had never done that. The day had been redeemed; she put out of her head the disturbing sight of the prisoners of war and the unwelcome Mitchells.

"We'd better keep the driving a secret," said Andrew when they were back in the boat. "I don't think Aunt Florence would appreciate it." They exchanged a grin. As the boat slowed down to approach the island Norah kept sneaking looks at Andrew. His clear eyes were fixed on Gairloch and a peaceful expression was on his face.

Now she could say it. She could whisper, "I love you, Andrew," the way women did in movies. Then he would reveal that he loved her too, that he always had but thought she was too young to tell.

But the *Putt-Putt* arrived at the dock while Norah was still trying to pick exactly the right moment. The picnickers were back. Gavin and Sally jumped up from their fishing rods to greet them and the family engulfed her once more.

12

The Party

"*T*he Elders want to see you, Flo," panted Janet. She had run all the way down from the cottage. "They're just finishing breakfast but they asked me to tell you to meet them in the living room in five minutes. What have you done?" she added curiously.

"Nothing!" Flo looked annoyed. "I wonder what they want. What a bother … I was just going to go to the mainland to get some more writing paper."

"Well, hurry up," said Janet. "Aunt Florence has that solemn look. I bet you *have* done something—something awful—and you won't tell us!"

She ducked to avoid Flo's pillow. Then they watched the tall girl meander up to the cottage, refusing to hurry.

"She sure has nerve," said Clare. "I wonder what's up."

Norah sat down heavily. "Maybe it's news—bad news! You know—about one of the boys she writes to."

They stared at her. "Oh, no," said Janet softly. "Oh, poor Flo …" Even Clare's face showed concern.

Norah twisted a corner of her sheet in her hands, the same choking fear filling her as in her nightmare about home. Last night, when Uncle Barclay had told her Churchill was in Canada for a conference, she had been irritated to be reminded once more about the war. Now its tentacles stretched toward them.

They sat on their unmade beds and waited. Then Janet leaned far out the window.

"She's coming! She's running and she doesn't look sad at all—she looks happy!"

Flo tore into the dorm and collapsed on her bed. "Listen everyone, I have *wonderful* news!" She glanced at their drained faces. "What's wrong?"

Janet bounced down beside her and gave her sister a squeeze. "Nothing!" she crowed. "Tell us!"

"Wait until you hear this. The Elders are abandoning us!"

"What?" Clare frowned. "Don't joke, Flo. This morning has been dramatic enough already."

"It's not a joke! You know that wedding they're all going to this Saturday."

They nodded. Aunt Anne's sister was getting married from the Royal Muskoka Hotel on one of the other lakes, and Sally was to be a flower girl.

"They were going to leave for the hotel on Saturday morning and come back the same day." Flo grinned. "Well, now they're staying overnight! They won't be back until Sunday evening because someone's having a lunch the next day."

"But that means—" began Janet.

"Exactly! We'll be alone. Andrew and I are in charge.

We'll have the whole island to ourselves for almost two days!"

"But what about the Hancocks?" said Norah.

"They're going away too! Their nephew is home on leave and they're taking the train back to Toronto for the weekend."

"It's not that great," said Clare. "Won't we have to babysit George and Denny? That will take all our time— you know what brats they can be."

"They're going to the wedding! Aunt Anne thinks they should see Sally being a flower girl and her relatives have arranged a sitter for them afterwards. So it will just be us! Of course, there are the other little boys, but they're easy enough to look after. Now listen, I have a wonderful idea—let's have a party!"

"Now you're talking!" said Clare. "On Saturday night?"

Flo nodded. "Andrew and I can ask all our friends and you may too, of course."

Janet looked worried. "Are we *allowed* to have a party?"

"Of course not, silly! But no one will know, because almost everyone's parents will be at the wedding too!"

"I don't think we should do it," said Janet primly. "What if the Elders find out? Imagine how furious Aunt Florence would be ..."

Flo grimaced but Clare said, "Don't be such a baby, Janet. We won't get caught, as long as we clean up after-wards. *I* think it's a swell idea. I've been waiting all summer for something exciting to happen and this is it!"

"It really will be all right, Janet," Flo reassured her

sister. "Let's make a list!" She tore a page from her writing pad. "We'll ask the Mackenzies, the Laziers, Ceci Johnson and her friend from the States … We'll have to spend the next few days going around in the boat and passing the word—we can pretend we're going on a lot of picnics."

"Make sure there aren't too many girls," warned Clare. "And I'll ask Louise to bring all her records."

Janet and Norah listened quietly, scarcely believing that they were included as well. Then Janet added a few names to the list. Norah didn't have any friends up north to ask but that didn't matter—she was beginning to feel excited.

"Flo, do you think Andrew will want to do it?" she dared to ask, not looking at Clare.

"Oh, I'm sure he will," said Flo. "Andrew always likes to have a good time. It'll be nice to plan something with him again, the way we used to. We won't be able to tell him until he gets back from the Mitchells', though." She looked wistful. "He's always over there."

"Make sure you ask Jamie and Dick," said Clare.

"What about Peter and Ross and Gavin? What if they tell?" said Janet.

"Janet, will you stop worrying!" said Clare. "I'll manage Peter and Ross. I know enough things they've done to threaten them with. How about Gavin, Norah—can you trust him?"

"Of course I can!" said Norah indignantly. "He won't say anything if I ask him not to, and I don't have to threaten him."

"We'll give them something to do so they feel part of it," said Flo. "I know—they can meet the boats and help tie them up. Now *food* ... we need another list."

FOR NORAH, the best part about preparing for the party was that Andrew was so enthusiastically involved. He stayed on the island and shared in their secret plans, even coming down to the boathouse at night to discuss them. He treated Norah to the same teasing banter that he did the other cousins; Norah was relieved that Clare didn't say anything.

While the cousins were keyed up with suppressed excitement about the party, the Elders were busy getting ready for the wedding.

"I'm sorry we have to leave you all behind, Norah," said Aunt Mary, as Norah helped her pin some new silk flowers on her hat. "It's going to be such a beautiful wedding—the wedding of the summer. But I suppose you'll like being on your own for a change."

"We will," Norah assured her. She wished she could tell Aunt Mary about the party; she was the only Elder who probably wouldn't mind.

"There!" Aunt Mary tweaked a bow on the hat. "That should match my new dress perfectly. I have to pick it up today."

Now that the dress was finished, Norah wondered what she'd use for an excuse to visit Tom. Would he be at the wedding? Would Aunt Mary have to pretend she didn't know him? Or perhaps they would decide that this was the occasion to announce their engagement. Quiet Aunt Mary was really the most romantic member of the family, Norah thought dreamily.

"Weddings! What a lot of fuss!" complained Aunt Catherine. Norah sat on the old woman's bed while she shook out an ancient beaded sweater and frowned at a moth hole in it. "They're bad enough in the winter but having to get all dressed up in the summer … I'm half-inclined to stay here with you young ones. I'm sure you'll have a better time than I will." She tugged on the sweater and grimaced at her reflection in the mirror.

"Oh," said Norah in a panic. But then Aunt Catherine added, "I have to go, though—the bride's parents are old friends. Weddings terrify me, you know."

"Why?"

"Because all my life I've had a recurring nightmare of standing in front of the altar and suddenly changing my mind—but not daring to say so because everyone would be disappointed. Whenever I see the bride and groom standing there I feel trapped. Much better to be independent, not saddled with someone for the rest of your life."

Norah was shocked. "But what about love?"

"Love!" Aunt Catherine chuckled. "Love's all very well, and none of us can do without it. We wouldn't want to, either. But it's like champagne—bubbly and sweet, but the effect doesn't last. Not the moonlight and roses kind of love, anyway. Look at our last king—Edward—where did love get him? It lost him the throne."

A dim memory stirred in Norah of sitting in the kitchen with her family, listening to the king's words from the wireless, words she had often heard grownups quote since then: that he could not be king "without the help and support of the woman I love."

"But why can't he marry her and still *be* king?" she had asked.

"Because she's divorced and they won't let him," Muriel had replied. "So he's sacrificing his throne for her. Isn't that romantic? It's true love ..."

"Love! Puh!" Grandad had sputtered. He had sounded very much like Aunt Catherine just now. "What's so important about love? It's *duty* that's important. The fellow is neglecting his duty."

"You loved Granny," Tibby had said gently.

"That's different—that's *marriage*," Grandad had retorted.

"Don't you think *anyone* should get married?" Norah asked Aunt Catherine now, more bewildered each second.

"You poor child—what have I been telling you? Of course marriage can be splendid for some people. Look at Dorothy and Barclay—they've always seemed to me to have a good steady relationship. Marriage works when all the romance nonsense ends and you learn to give each other space and respect. But it's not for me. Everyone doesn't *have* to marry, you know. I could have, several times. But I'm just as happy—probably happier—alone. Not that anyone is going to propose to me now!" She struggled out of the sweater and shook herself like a small, fierce terrier. "But don't listen to the ramblings of an old woman, Norah. You'll fall in love one day and you might get married too. Just make sure you do what you want to do."

Norah walked slowly downstairs. She had always thought that Aunt Catherine wasn't married because no one had ever asked her. But to deliberately choose not to be … And she *was* happy, there was no denying that. Happier than some of the aunts, like Aunt Mar, who seemed only half-here with Uncle Peter away, or Aunt Anne, who fussed so much about being a perfect wife. But her own parents—now that she thought of it—had always seemed to be contented with each other. She wondered if Muriel and Barry would be.

Andrew waved to her as he walked by on the veran-dah. Norah's heart danced and she forgot her unsettling reflections. It seemed to her that love was much simpler than Aunt Catherine made out—and of course, *she* wanted to get married.

"GOODBYE! Have a good time!" All the cousins stood on the dock and waved cheerfully. Uncle Gerald and his family had already left with a neighbour and the eight remaining Elders were crammed into the *Florence,* with Uncle Barclay at the wheel.

"They look like people in the movies," Gavin whispered to Norah. With their festive hats, bright floral-printed dresses, strings of pearls and crisp suits the aunts and uncles glittered with importance. A long time later, whenever

Norah thought of the Elders she remembered them like this: "dressed to the nines," as Aunt Catherine said, looking as proud and excited as children going on an outing.

"Take good care of Bosley, Gavin," said Uncle Reg.

"You are only to leave the island for an emergency," said Aunt Florence.

"And remember, Flo—no visitors," added Aunt Dorothy. In the noisy farewells, Flo managed not to answer.

"Behave yourselves!" were the last words they heard. They waved dutifully until the launch was out of sight; then they grinned at each other.

"We're free!" laughed Flo. "Let's get going. Andrew, you have the list of food to get. The rest of you come up and start moving furniture."

By NOON, when Andrew had returned from Ford's Bay with cartons of Orange Crush and Coke and packages of crackers and peanuts, the cottage was ready. All the living-room furniture had been pushed to the sides or put out onto the verandah. The rugs had been rolled up, leaving a bare expanse of painted floorboards. A stack of records lay ready by the new phonograph.

The little boys had listened solemnly while Flo told them about the party. "If you say anything, Peter and Ross, I'll tell Mother you were the ones who broke her sewing machine," said Clare.

"Don't worry—we'll never tell!" said Gavin earnestly. The three of them beamed with the honour of being included.

They all helped spread the crackers with cheese and a dab of jelly and arrange them on plates. Then Flo cooked them a huge batch of corn-on-the-cob for lunch. They devoured it in minutes, their faces gleaming with butter.

"Hanny will notice we've used all the butter ration," said Janet.

"We'll just do without it for the rest of the weekend," Flo told her.

"Come on, you three—I'll take you fishing in the rowboat while the women make themselves beautiful," said Andrew. Gavin, Peter and Ross ran after him.

As soon as the boys had left, the girls went skinny-dipping off the dock, playing catch with the floating bar of soap. Then they washed their hair in the lake. Norah watched the other three put their hair up in pincurls.

"Shall I do yours too?" Flo asked her.

Norah wasn't sure how different she wanted to look, but she decided to risk it. Flo carefully twisted squiggly shapes all over her head. The four of them sat in a row to dry their hair and Flo began to shave her legs.

"Let me try," said Clare. "Mother says I'm too young, but if I start she won't be able to do anything about it."

Norah and Janet watched closely while Clare soaped one leg and drew the razor along it, leaving a gleaming bare patch.

"Ouch!" A line of red welled up. "Now look what I've done!" Clare splashed water on her leg to stop the bleeding but she had to press a wet towel on the cut.

"I'm glad I don't have to shave my legs yet," Janet whispered to Norah. "Mum says I'm so blonde I may never have to."

Norah looked down at her own smooth legs and gingerly touched the metal layer of bobby pins on her head. They were hot from the sun and they pinched. She let Janet paint the nails on her toes and fingers a shiny red and began to feel she was in disguise.

For the next hour they examined their clothes, trying on and trading until each person was satisfied. Flo passed around a jar of Odo-ro-no. "You don't want to have BO—the dancing will make you perspire," she warned. Then Flo and Clare covered their legs with some brown liquid called Velva Leg Film. Janet wanted some too, but there wasn't enough.

"I wish it wasn't so hard to get stockings," she grumbled. "You're lucky your legs are so brown, Norah. Mine are so white and freckled. And I look so *fat* ..."

She did look fat—in her flowered print dress cinched at the waist, she resembled a sausage tied in the middle.

"You look ... *curvy*," said Norah desperately. "Sort of like Dorothy Lamour."

"You look perfectly all right," said Flo. "And the point is not to worry about your appearance—just to have a good time. Now it's your turn, Norah."

After Norah had her dress on—an old one of Clare's that she had reluctantly lent her—Flo brushed out her hair and tied a blue bow on one side. Then she carefully applied some of her Tangee lipstick to Norah's open mouth.

"Wow! Have a look!" Norah went over and stood in front of the cracked mirror on the back of the door. The others gathered behind her as she drew in her breath with surprise.

Her hair was its usual dull brown, but now the ends burst into a froth that tickled her cheeks. The ribbon drew attention away from her nose. Her red mouth made her teeth look very white. Her dress was tight to the waist, then fell in soft folds, with Janet's silver pumps gleaming underneath.

"You're beautiful!" smiled Flo. "It's incredible—you could pass for sixteen at least."

"Oh, Norah, I wish I could look like that!" cried Janet. Clare didn't say anything but her pursed mouth looked grudgingly approving.

Norah crossed her arms over her chest. "Do you—do you think I need a bra? I'm getting one in the fall."

"That tight dress is fine without one," said Flo.

Norah let her arms hang free and continued to stare at the stranger in the mirror. Was that *her*? She smiled at her reflection and it grinned saucily back. What would Andrew think?

"Now there are fifteen!" panted Gavin. He collapsed beside Norah on the verandah swing, after racing full speed up the hill. He was almost hysterical with excitement; his eyes glittered and his cheeks were flushed a deep red. Aunt Florence would have called him overwrought and sent him to bed, but Norah didn't want to spoil his obvious enjoyment of the party. "Ten launches, three rowboats and two canoes," continued Gavin. "Peter and Ross are still helping tie them up."

All evening the little boys had greeted the boats and pointed the guests towards the party. That was unnecessary: the steps were dotted with candles and above them Gairloch's glowing windows beamed like a lighthouse into the darkness. Out of them drifted the strains of the Glenn Miller band, overladen with laughing chatter.

Teen-agers spilled out of the house onto the verandah, perching on the railing with cigarettes, bottles of pop or the beer that some of them had brought. Norah was studying a couple who were kissing close to her. The boy dived into the girl's neck; he seemed to be nibbling on it. Norah continued to stare as the couple's heads twisted and turned. "Necking" was a very accurate description, she decided. It didn't look very comfortable.

"Whoops—here comes another one!" Gavin tumbled down to the dock again as the lights of a launch streamed across the lake. Norah went over to the railing and gazed at the flotilla of boats, some tied to the dock and some to each other.

She wiped her sweaty palms on the skirt of her dress, took a deep breath, and plunged into the party again. She had only lasted a few minutes on her last attempt. Three times the noise and the grown-upness had overwhelmed her and she'd escaped to breathe more easily on the verandah.

Norah found Janet hugging Bosley on the windowseat, a dreamy look on her face. "Someone asked me to dance!" she whispered with awe.

Norah squished in beside her. "*Who?* Did you?"

Janet nodded solemnly and pointed. "With that boy over there—the one with glasses. He's Louise's cousin. But I stepped on his foot, so we stopped. I don't mind though—at least I was asked! I never have been before."

"What's his name?" The boy was sitting on the far side of the room, guzzling a Coke. He caught their eyes and scuttled out of the room.

"Now we've scared him away," sighed Janet. "Oh well. His name is Mark and he's only staying in Muskoka for another two days. I asked him lots of questions to draw him out, the way it says in *Ladies' Home Journal,* but he didn't seem to want to answer them."

"You were so brave to say yes," said Norah. "I hope no one asks *me* to dance. It would be so embarrassing."

"Have some peanuts." Janet had a bowl of them beside her. The two of them ate them all, throwing an occasional tidbit to Bosley, while they watched the party. Couples—some mixed and many consisting of two girls—jitterbugged before them, waggling their hands and almost leaping off the ground with energy. Some of the girls were dancing so hard that their leg make-up ran down in streaks; occasionally one would be lifted high above the crowd or swooped between her partner's legs. The cat collection shook precariously on the mantelpiece as the whole room seemed to jump and sway. The hot space was filled with a smell of cigarette smoke and sweat.

"Shall we?" suggested Janet.

"I'm not very good," said Norah.

"Well, you know I'm not. We should practise and maybe then I'll stop stepping on people's feet."

They slid off the seat and began to jitterbug. They had often practised dancing in the boathouse, but here it was different. Norah was sure everyone in the room was eyeing them scornfully. Her arms felt wooden and her feet kept stepping out of Janet's shoes. "That's enough," she said finally. "I'd rather watch." Janet seemed quite willing to stop and they went back to their post.

Norah had lost track of Andrew; the last time she'd seen him he'd been helping Flo uncap more bottles. Now she spotted him again and frowned. He was dancing with Lois; she hadn't even noticed the Mitchells arrive. Lois was teasing him about something, poking his chest while they danced. Andrew's deep answering laugh made Norah's insides lurch with jealousy. He had said hello to her in passing but he hadn't said anything about how she looked.

Someone put on "Stardust." The mixed couples came together like magnets and the single girls retreated to the sides of the room. Some of the couples kissed while they danced, barely moving to the hypnotic melody.

"Slow ones are such a bore," said Janet. "Look at Clare! Who's she with?"

Clare was snuggled into the shoulder of a tall blond boy.

"Aunt Mar wouldn't like that," said Janet. "He's too old for her." Then Flo steered a giggling Peter past them and they all laughed.

"Why are most of the girls older than the boys?" asked Norah suddenly. Some of the girls were as sophisticated-looking as movie stars, but many of the boys had skin pocked with acne and gangly arms and legs.

"Because the older boys are all in the war, silly."

Of course; now she remembered Flo saying how many of her friends were also writing letters to the front. Andrew and Clare's partner were the oldest. Norah let herself look at Andrew again; Lois was holding him so close Norah couldn't stand it.

"I need some air," she whispered, and slipped out into the night.

Gavin was on the glider, fast asleep. She half-carried him, half-led him to bed. Then she spent the next few hours swinging in her chair in time to the music, falling into a light sleep, then jerking awake again. She could go to bed herself, but she liked taking advantage of the fact that there was no one to tell her to. And she couldn't seem to leave the party; it was as if it were going to go on forever and she was stuck in it like a trance.

One after another the velvety melodies floated out to her: "Blue Moon," "Moonlight Serenade," and the whirling crescendo of "In the Mood." Again and again someone put on "You'll Never Know." That's *our* song, Norah decided. Most of the songs were about moons and dreams and partings and they all had a wistful edge to them. Being grown-up seemed to be one endless love scene where someone was in love and the other had left or didn't return the love.

Andrew's voice very close to her startled her awake. A strident female one answered it. "Come on, Andrew, just a short ride. *Why* can't you?"

Andrew and Lois were standing at the top of the verandah steps. Norah kept very still, rubbing her eyes. She must have slept for a long time. Now the party seemed to be ending; down by the water voices were calling out goodbyes.

"I told you," said Andrew, sounding as if he were controlling his impatience. "I'm supposed to be in charge and I don't want to leave my cousins alone."

"For Pete's sake, they're not babies! Can't we just nip over to Little Island? We'd have it all to ourselves. I'm beginning to think you're afraid of me."

They moved down the steps and into the shadows right below her. There was a long silence during which Norah, embarrassed and furious, hunched farther into the glider. She could see by their outline that they were locked in an embrace.

"There! Now will you take me?" wheedled Lois.

"Lois ... " said Andrew, as if he were entreating her not to keep asking. Then a voice below called her name as well. "Lois! Are you coming or not?"

"There!" said Andrew eagerly. "Jamie and Dick are leaving—you'd better go with them."

"Oh, all right," grumbled Lois. "Sometimes you're a spoilsport, Andrew."

Norah leaned over the railing as the two of them went hand in hand down the steps. She listened to Andrew call goodbye, and sighed with relief as the boat carrying Lois chugged away.

13

A Promise

N orah expected Andrew to return to the party—
there were still a few lingering dancers—but he
strode around the side of the cottage. She slipped off the
verandah and set out along the path by the lake to trail
him.

After her sleep she was rested and alert. She had left
behind her uncomfortable shoes and undone the pinch-
ing ribbon from her hair. The night air was warm and
soft. A whippoorwill trilled its endless refrain, a startled
raccoon lumbered out of her way and a few bats swooped
in front of her. Crickets chirped in a reedy chorus. Norah
slid through the lively darkness like a fish through water,
her head up to admire the glittering sky. This was as
magical and romantic a night as in the songs.

Finally she spotted Andrew, a dark, seated figure high
up on her lookout. Norah stole through the trees and
paused at the base of the rock. She could slip away again
without him hearing her, but that would be cowardly.

"Andrew," Norah called.

He jerked around. "Who's there?"

"It's me—Norah."

"Norah! I thought you'd be in bed by now. Come and share the view—it's such a beautiful night."

Carefully Norah's toes found the footholds that were so familiar to her in daylight. She trembled with pleasure as Andrew reached out and took her hand.

"Thanks," she mumbled, flopping down beside him. Her cheeks were burning so much, she was glad it was dark. The rock still gave off a faint glow of heat from the day.

"This used to be my favourite place when I was younger," said Andrew.

"Did it? It's *my* favourite place!" Norah was so pleased, she forgot to feel awkward.

"I know—I've seen you up here."

Had he seen her spying on him? But Andrew was smiling. His eyes, dim by moonlight, were concentrating only on her.

"I meant to tell you how pretty you look tonight, Norah. Have you done something different with your hair?"

"Flo curled it," mumbled Norah.

"Hmmm … maybe you should do it like that all the time."

"It's too much trouble! I might later—when I'm sixteen or so."

"You'll probably be back in England when you're sixteen," said Andrew. "Surely the war will be over by then. Now that Sicily has been taken, it looks a lot more hopeful."

He didn't sound hopeful. He sounded, Norah realized, absolutely miserable. She remembered the night she'd seen him crying.

"Are you upset that the war might be over before you can be in it?" she asked carefully.

Andrew gave a dry, mocking laugh. "It's kind of the opposite. I'm afraid the war might *not* be over and I'll have to fight in it."

Norah swallowed hard. "Don't you want to, then?"

Andrew whirled around so fast that Norah gasped. "No, I do not! I've never wanted to do anything less in my entire life!" He leaned over and grabbed Norah's shoulders. "I don't *want* to kill anyone! I don't think it's right! But do you think my parents or anyone else in this damned family understands that?"

Andrew dropped his hands and Norah controlled the impulse to rub the painful places where he'd gripped her.

Andrew sighed. "I'm sorry, Norah. I didn't mean to scare you. Now you know. You're the only person I've ever told. I guess you're the only one I *can* tell, since you're not really part of the family. But I shouldn't bother you with my problems. I'm sorry," he said again. He sounded as if he were going to cry.

"It's okay," whispered Norah. "I don't mind." They were quiet for what seemed like an eternity, Andrew's fierce words echoing in the darkness.

"Aunt Catherine said that too," said Norah slowly. "She said that you weren't cut out to be a soldier and that you were born at the wrong time."

"Aunt Catherine is the only one who understands," said Andrew. "You know how kids play Cowboys and Indians and pretend to shoot each other? I never did—I used to pretend that my gun was a camera! It really upset my father—he was always buying me new, bigger guns to entice me. And I hated Cadets—all that stupid drilling. Do you know how many men were killed at Dieppe?"

"How many?" whispered Norah. She remembered the horror all the grown-ups had felt last August when so many Canadians had been lost. But she and the other cousins had been so busy playing games they hadn't paid much attention.

"Almost nine hundred! Think of that! Nine hundred men slaughtered like cattle—for what? Doesn't it seem intolerable and absurd to you that whenever human beings disagree they go out and *kill* each other?" His arms thrust wildly as his words rushed out.

Norah's head was whirling, but she tried to keep it above Andrew's rising passion.

"But what about *Hitler*? Don't we have to beat him?"

Beating Hitler had been ingrained in Norah's consciousness since she was nine. She remembered her own efforts to help. "I used to watch for his planes in England," she said softly. "All my friends did. We thought the war was fun then. I don't any more, but I still think we have to fight him. What would happen if he won?" Her voice rose in panic. "What would happen to *England*? And to my family?"

Andrew patted her knee. "You're perfectly right, Norah—don't worry. I know we have to beat him so people like your family can be safe. And we probably will. It's just too bad that war seems to be the only way." He sighed. "I feel like such a freak. Every one of my friends seems to take it for granted we'll all join up. Even fellows as bright as my friend Jack seem to be able to stomach it. We had a terrible argument the night before he left—*he* thinks I should fight. I don't know anyone who feels the way I do."

Norah was trying very hard not to think of Andrew as a freak herself. She'd never heard anyone express any doubts about the war—except for Aunt Catherine. But Andrew was a *man,* not an old woman. "Are you afraid?" Norah asked, almost angrily.

"I've thought about that a lot," said Andrew slowly. "I guess everyone must be afraid—you wouldn't be human if you weren't. But I think you could make yourself do it when the crunch comes—'screw your courage to the sticking place' and all that. I *could* do that, I think— but it doesn't seem morally right to me. So I feel like such a phoney, with everyone thinking I'm going off to learn how to be an officer and then maybe join the war."

"But it's only maybe," Norah reminded him. "You might not even have to."

"Yes, I could avoid it—but don't you see how that makes me even more of a phoney? I'm not taking any sort of stand—everyone thinks I'm eager to get in on it, as Uncle Barclay keeps saying. If I'm lucky I won't have to fight, but then I'll spend the rest of my life pretending to be sorry I didn't. I just can't live that sort of lie!"

Norah listened to the pain in his voice. There was no way she could argue with his conviction.

She took a deep breath. All right, then. No matter how much she disagreed with him, she would accept his beliefs, if that was what loving him demanded.

"What do you *want* to do?" she asked.

"I want to be an actor, of course," said Andrew at once. "I want to do it *now*, not wait until after the war— to quit university and try to get on with some company."

"What would happen if you did that? Would someone make you fight anyway?"

"When I'm older I'd have to do service here in Canada, but they wouldn't make me go overseas. Do you know what they call guys like that? 'Zombies.' Can you imagine how the family would feel if I was a zombie? Their golden boy, their Hugh, being such a coward …"

All at once Norah saw everything very clearly. She felt older, not younger, than Andrew. "That wouldn't be being a coward!" she said firmly. "Standing up for what you believe in would be braver than fighting." She got up on her knees with excitement. "It doesn't *matter* what they think, Andrew! You should do what you want! It's not what I would do, or Flo or Uncle Barclay or most other people— but it's what *you* should do. Just tell them that you're never going to fight, so it's no use taking that course! Just tell them!" She didn't even realize she was shaking his arm.

Her face was so close that she could see his expression clearly—as if he were afraid of her. Then he threw back his head and laughed, laughter that was very close to crying.

"Oh, Norah, you are a wonder," he said, wiping his eyes. "*You'd* tell them, wouldn't you? You're much braver than I am. And of course, you're right. What you're suggesting is what I've been struggling with all summer. I *should* tell them and do what I want—but I don't know if I can! Isn't it ridiculous? I'm more frightened of this family than I am of the war!"

"Of course you can!" cried Norah. "Tell them tomorrow! Will you?"

Andrew shuddered. "Not tomorrow!" He was quiet again, and then he said slowly, "But maybe ... yes, I will tell them, and very soon. I'll have to wait for exactly the right moment—when we're all together and I've worked up enough courage. Perhaps on our last night—then I can escape the repercussions. And believe me, there'll be plenty of them! I've been thinking that if I *did* decide to do this, I could live with some friends in Saskatchewan. There's a student company there I could try to join."

"But you'll do it? Do you promise?"

Andrew laughed again, but this time it was joyful. "Yes, I promise I'll do it. Thank you, Norah—you've helped me make up my mind. I was beginning to feel frozen—as if I'd *never* decide."

Norah thought she would burst with pleasure. "You're very welcome," she grinned.

"We'd better go—the others must be wondering why you're not in bed. I'll go down and make sure everyone's left." Andrew took her hand again as they stumbled down the rock.

"Good-night," whispered Norah. She flew down to the boathouse, her arms spread wide as if she were a bird. Minutes later, as she lay in bed and went over each burning word of their conversation, she realized she hadn't fulfilled her aim—she hadn't told him she loved him. But that could wait a while. Andrew had revealed his most intimate feelings to her. And he had entrusted her with an important secret. Surely that meant he felt something for her too.

14

Up the River

"*P*lease pass the peanuts," said Gavin solemnly.

"And the pickles," giggled Ross. He sandwiched a pickle between two crackers and crammed it into his mouth. "Yummy! I wish we had this kind of breakfast every day!"

Flo yawned, had a sip of coffee and grimaced. "What did you put in this, Andrew? It doesn't taste like Hanny's."

Even though it was eleven, they were sprawled around the kitchen table in their pyjamas. Flo had begun by setting out bowls and a box of cereal, but the little boys had discovered the leftover food and now they were all enjoying it. The kitchen was a disaster: empty bottles, cigarette boxes and glasses took up every bit of space on the counters. The windows were wide open to get rid of the smoky smell.

"What a terrific party," sighed Clare. "Everyone said it was the best one of the summer."

"It was," agreed Flo. "I didn't realize so many people would come. Who *were* they all?"

"Friends of friends," grinned Andrew. "Word must have spread quickly. Some people even came from Huntsville!"

Flo turned to Clare. "Who was that boy *you* were with? He seemed a bit old for you."

Clare bristled. "He's not that old—twenty-two."

"Twenty-two!" gasped Janet, but Clare ignored her. "He's in the Norwegian Airforce. He's been training at the Muskoka Airport but he's leaving tomorrow so I won't be able to see him again. But he asked me to write to him," she added smugly. "Now I'll have someone in the war too."

"What about your boy friend in Montreal—what will *he* think?" Janet asked her.

"He can think what he wants. After all, Flo writes to more than one boy. Like she says, fellows who are overseas need to be cheered up."

Norah glanced at Andrew. He caught her eye and winked back; Clare's comments didn't seem to be bothering him.

"You just want someone to boast about," said Janet. "I don't think your mother is going to like you writing to someone so old. *I* enjoyed the dancing the most," she added, as if everyone had asked her. "Mark and I had a swell time trying the foxtrot."

Norah didn't think Mark had asked Janet to dance again, but she didn't say anything. She felt warm inside, as if a bright flame were burning steadily. In a blissful daze she listened to Andrew tease Janet about having a boy friend. Everything about this morning was special and new. She ran her hands over the smooth scrubbed pine of the table and took another delicious sip of Orange Crush out of its brown ribbed bottle.

They all lingered until Flo glanced at her watch. She leapt up. "It's almost noon! They'll be back in five hours! All right, everyone, we have to begin. Janet, you empty all the ashtrays. Norah and Clare, bring everything in from the living room and Andrew can put back the furniture. I'll start on the kitchen. You three boys scour every inch of the island for litter—especially cigarette butts!"

By four-thirty no one would have guessed there had been a huge party at Gairloch the night before. All of the living room furniture was back in its usual place. Every surface in the kitchen gleamed. They had burned most of the garbage and hidden the bottles for Andrew to sneak over to Ford's Bay the next day.

They sat in a row on the dock, drooping with sleepiness while they waited for the launch.

"No more freedom," complained Clare, when Peter sighted the boats. "Remember," she warned her brothers. "Not a word! I can hardly wait until I'm old enough to leave home and have parties whenever I want to."

"I wish we had just one more day," sighed Flo. "I love the feeling of having the island all to ourselves."

"It'll be fun to hear about the wedding, though," said Janet.

"Maybe they'll bring us presents!" added Ross. He jumped up and waved as the boat came closer.

The clan swarmed onto the dock and the usual kissing and exclamations began. Norah submitted to it all cheerfully.

"Look how neat and tidy everything is!" said Aunt Dorothy when they reached the cottage.

"We cleaned the whole cottage as a surprise," said Flo quickly. "It gave us something to do."

Everyone sat in the living room, the children exchanging guilty looks as the Elders praised them. Politely they listened to all the different versions of the wedding.

"Sally was the star," said her mother fondly. "She looked so adorable and she even sang a song at the reception, didn't you sweetheart?"

"I didn't want to," said Sally indignantly. "I only did it because you asked me to."

"But didn't you like being a flower girl?" Clare asked her.

"It was okay. But there was so much *waiting*."

Each of the children was given a thin slice of wedding cake. "I don't know how they managed such a big cake," said Aunt Dorothy. "Put it under your pillows tonight and whoever you dream of is the one you'll marry."

"I'm not *getting* married, so I may as well eat mine now," said Peter. All the Elders laughed as he gulped down his cake in one bite.

But Norah saved hers carefully. That night she went to bed early, but before she fell asleep she remembered to place the cake, wrapped in its paper doily, under her pillow. She always thought of Andrew last thing at night anyway, so she knew she'd dream about him.

THE NEXT MORNING she sat up in bed, nibbling thoughtfully at her flattened piece of cake. She had slept so soundly she couldn't remember her dreams. The other girls smiled secretly and said they wouldn't tell who they had dreamed about; Norah suspected they had forgotten as well.

She lay back in bed and nestled in her cosy blankets.

Andrew tells the family he isn't going to university and he's never going to join up. Then he goes to Saskatchewan and becomes the most promising actor in Canada. When the war is over he moves to England and begins acting there, so he can live close to Norah until she's old enough to marry ...

Sally wandered in. "Hanny wants to know why you haven't come to breakfast yet."

"We're *tired*," giggled Janet. "But we can't tell you why."

"*I* know why. You had a party! Ross told me."

"I'll throttle him!" said Clare. "You'd better not tell, Sally!"

Sally looked at her slyly. "If you let me borrow your ukelele for the rest of the summer, then I won't tell."

"All right," sighed Clare. "But don't play it now," she protested, as the little girl began to strum the ukelele. "I want to put on a record."

They all lay back in their beds as the song began. "I'll be seeing you / In all the old familiar places ..." Sally got into bed with Flo and the older girl whispered to her about keeping the party a secret.

"I'll be looking at the moon / But I'll be seeing you." The melody lingered in the air after the song was over.

"Don't put that one on again, Clare," said Flo. "It makes me miss Ned too much."

"I wonder if I'll ever see Gunnar again," mused Clare.

"And Mark …" Janet said mournfully.

Norah tried to feel sad. Now that Andrew was going to Saskatchewan she wouldn't see him in Toronto this fall. When *would* she see him? But she couldn't seem to think beyond this blissful present, with his confiding words still ringing in her ears.

"I'm sure glad I'm not sleeping in here any more," declared Sally. "You're *still* talking about love."

"What should we do today? Everything seems so flat after the party," complained Clare. "And Louise has gone back to the city—I have no one to visit."

"Mum says I have to do some math," moaned Janet. "I have a whole workbook to get through. It's almost the end of the summer and I haven't even started it! Would you help me, Norah? You're so good at math."

Norah sat up again and looked out at the bright blue lake. It was much too inviting a morning to waste on schoolwork. And the summer *was* ending, she realized with alarm—only two more weeks! She wanted to do something special, something she'd never done before. Not with Andrew—now that she felt so sure of him she needed a rest from his intensity.

"No thanks, Janet," she said, as nicely as she could. "I have other plans."

"'I have other plans'—what plans?" Clare mimicked her accent but Norah ignored her as she hurried into her clothes and ran up the steps.

"Good-morning, Aunt Florence," she said politely as, ten minutes later, she placed Aunt Florence's breakfast on her guardian's lap.

"Oh, it's you, Norah. Where's Gavin this morning?"

"He'll come up and take your tray. I wanted to ask you something."

"Well, ask away." Aunt Florence poured out her tea and leaned back against her plump pillows, looking as if she were already preparing to say no.

"Do you think Gavin and I could go somewhere today? On our own, I mean. The lake's very calm. I thought I could take him in the *Putt-Putt* to Mirror River and then go up it in the canoe—we could tow it behind on the way, like we did two years ago with Uncle Gerald."

"All the way to Mirror River? By yourselves? I don't think so, Norah. If you want to get Flo or Andrew to take you, that would be fine."

"But—" Norah tried to stay polite. "You see, this week is our anniversary."

Aunt Florence looked amused. "Your what?"

"Our anniversary. It's three years ago this week that we left England."

"Why so it is! I'd forgotten. It seems much longer than three years. I feel as if you've always been with us." She smiled fondly at Norah.

Encouraged, Norah smiled back. "I thought it would be nice if Gavin and I went somewhere by ourselves," she continued. "Sometimes I worry that he's forgotten about

home. If we spent all day talking about it, he'd remember
more."

That wasn't the real reason Norah wanted to go; she
just felt like an adventure. And she'd been so obsessed
with Andrew lately; Gavin *did* deserve some of her time.
She put on her best responsible-elder-sister role and
waited.

Aunt Florence finished a piece of toast. "That's a very
nice idea, Norah. And you'd probably like a holiday from
all of us—I imagine that you sometimes find this family a
bit overwhelming. But couldn't you just go to Little
Island? Mirror River is quite a long journey. If it were just
you and Janet I'd say yes, but I can't have you taking your
little brother that far. What if you had engine trouble—
or the weather changed? Remember how Mr. Hancock
and Gerald were caught in that fog last summer and had
to spend all night on the lake."

Norah couldn't see how these dangers would be any
worse with Gavin than with Flo or Janet. She knew the
real reason—Gavin was too precious to Aunt Florence for
her to risk it. She swallowed the jealousy she'd felt when
she'd first arrived in Canada and Aunt Florence had
favoured Gavin, then continued to try reasonable arguments.

Finally Aunt Florence compromised. If Norah could
find an adult to take her and Gavin to the mouth of the
river, they could be left alone there for the day with the
canoe. Norah knew she wouldn't give in any more.

"BE SURE to keep your life-jackets on," said Aunt Florence, standing on the dock to see them off. "Wear your sun hats and be very, *very* careful. Gavin, you are to do exactly as Norah says." She kissed him and handed him the lunch Hanny had packed.

"Don't worry—we'll be careful. Goodbye!" Norah called. Uncle Gerald backed out the *Putt-Putt* and they waved to Aunt Florence, Janet and Sally, all gazing plaintively after them.

Gavin hunched in the stern in his bulky life-jacket, his face radiant. Norah perched in the middle. Around them bobbed a few white sails, barely moving in the still air. Uncle Gerald drove slowly to avoid upsetting the canoe, which bounced behind them.

Gavin began a favourite game—counting islands. Big or small, they were all a smudge of grey rock topped by dark firs. Some had cottages on them but most were uninhabited. Norah studied the mainland cottages they passed. Many were grander than Gairloch, with low stone walls and two, or even three, boathouses hung with geraniums.

When they reached Eden House Resort, Norah and Gavin exchanged a conspiratorial look. They passed through the cut at Port Schofield and entered the other lake.

"Look!" cried Gavin. Close to the boat swam a deer. Its branched head ploughed beside them for a while as if it were having a race. Then it turned towards the shore.

"Poor *thing*!" said Gavin. "It's tired! Maybe it won't make it."

"Deer are good swimmers," Uncle Gerald assured him. "It's probably enjoying itself!" But Gavin kept his eyes on the deer until it was a tiny dot behind them.

Finally they reached the mouth of Mirror River. Uncle Gerald emptied the water out of the canoe, lowered it into the inlet and helped them load it. "I'll meet you right here at four," he said. "Have you got a watch?"

Norah nodded. After she and Gavin watched the launch zoom away, they grinned at each other and got into the canoe. "You can try steering," said Norah. She picked up her paddle and the canoe nosed up the river as if it were as eager to explore as they were.

Mirror River was aptly named. Its glassy surface reproduced exactly the surrounding foliage and sky. The water was so shallow in parts that the canoe barely skimmed the bottom. "We certainly don't need these!" laughed Norah, shucking off her life-jacket.

They rounded a few bends and the scenery and its reflections merged so seamlessly that Norah almost felt dizzy. Every leaf of the towering treetops was etched below; white and yellow lilies, soft brown cat-tails and delicate ferns were all part of the shifting picture on the surface.

I'm so *lucky*, thought Norah, to have come to a place in Canada where I can be in a boat on a river. Gavin was humming one of his odd little songs and they paddled dreamily in unison. A few other canoes passed them, their occupants calling out cheerful hellos.

"How long until lunch?" asked Gavin finally.

"There's no shore to sit on. Let's tie up and walk until we find a picnic spot." Hiding the canoe in some bulrushes, they took out the lunch basket and swished through a meadow.

"There!" pointed Norah. Ahead of them rose a grassy hill, crowned with a clump of aspens. The ground beneath the trees was cushioned with moss and they could see as far as the lake.

"This is like our own private lookout," said Gavin, digging out the sandwiches.

As usual, Hanny had packed a feast. Egg sandwiches and chicken sandwiches, carrot sticks and apples, and half a blueberry pie. They finished it all.

Gavin lay on his back and burped. "I don't ever want to go back to school," he said. "I want to stay up north forever and ever."

"Mmm …" agreed Norah, turning over on her back too. The trees formed a dappled canopy above them. "Let's not even *think* about school." She gazed up into the leaves and drifted into another daydream about Andrew.

"You look like a lady," remarked Gavin, glancing at her blouse.

Norah blushed. "I'm a teen-ager," she told her brother. "Everyone starts to look different then. You will too, some day. You'll have to shave, like Andrew!"

Gavin chuckled. "Andrew's not very good at shaving—he's always cutting himself."

Norah remembered why she had told Aunt Florence they wanted this day by themselves. "Gavin," she said, sitting up and looking at him. "Do you realize it's three years ago that we left England? You were only five! Do you remember?" A picture flashed in her mind of their peaceful, wooded village, surrounded by hop gardens and orchards. So different from this raw landscape, but just as beautiful. For the first time since the letter from home she felt a pang of homesickness.

Gavin thought carefully. "I sort of remember it … I remember going on the boat. Who was that lady who took care of me? She let me hold her baby."

Norah frowned. "Mrs. Pym," she said quickly. Mrs. Pym had taken care of Gavin because Norah had been neglecting him.

"I remember when Aunt Florence gave me a little airplane when I got here. And I remember when we ran away—but then we came back. *Why* did we run away?"

"Oh, I don't know," said Norah. Gavin was remembering the wrong things—all the confusion and misery of their first few months in Canada. "I meant, what do you remember about *home*? Do you remember Little Whitebull?"

"What's that?"

"Gavin! It's our *house*! It has a green door and chickens in the yard." The painful place inside her throbbed at the memory of the chickens; it had been her job to feed them.

"Mum talked about those chickens in her last letter."

Norah remembered something. "*Muv*. That used to be your special name for her. Why don't you call her that any more?"

Gavin looked confused. "I don't call her *anything*. I never see her!"

"How do you begin your letters?" asked Norah.

"'Dear Mum and Dad'", said Gavin timidly. "That's how I've always started them, ever since I learned to print."

"Well, I think you should start saying 'Muv' again. She'd like that." Norah stared at her little brother for a second, then added gently, "Do you *really* remember them? Mum and Dad and Grandad and Muriel and Tibby? Of course, neither of us knows Barry."

Gavin looked defensive. "Of course I do! They're our *family*! They live in England!"

Norah sighed and stopped nagging him. Sometimes the features of her family's faces grew fuzzy in her own mind. And since she'd been in love with Andrew she'd hardly thought of them. Gavin must think of them even less, if at all. To him, Mum and Dad were the "family in England" that he wrote to automatically when Aunt Florence reminded him.

"You know…," she said slowly, hardly wanting to think about it herself, "some of the war guests are already starting to go back to England. Uncle Barclay read me a bit out of the paper. They think it's safe enough to go back now, even though the war isn't over."

"Go back to England!" Gavin sat up, looking scared. "Do *we* have to go back?"

"We won't go back until the war *is* over, because we were sponsored by the government and they won't pay for our passage until then. It's just the rich kids who are going back—the ones who can afford it."

"Aunt Florence could afford it ..." began Gavin. Then he laughed. "*She'd* never send us back."

He looked so relieved that Norah hated what she had to say next. "But you know we *are* going back some day, don't you? Aunt Florence can't keep us forever. We have to live with our real family—with Mum and Dad and Grandad, in Little Whitebull. In Ringden." She felt as if her words were stabbing him, but they rushed out anyway.

Gavin's big eyes filled with tears that beaded on his lashes. He looked at Norah imploringly. "And never come to Gairloch again? And leave our house in Toronto? And Roger and Tim?" Those were his special friends at school.

"Oh, Gavin ..." Norah patted him awkwardly. "I'm afraid so. But probably not for a few years."

"A few years is a long time," said Gavin desperately. "A *very* long time." He tried to smile at her.

They stared at each other helplessly. The future—that time "after the war" that the grown-ups kept talking about like a promised land—seemed unreal compared to this perfect day full of sunshine and gleaming water. At least Norah could daydream about Andrew meeting her in England—and she did want to see her family again. But now she realized how hard it was going to be for Gavin. He had always been more at home in Canada than she had.

"Let's not talk about going back to England any more, okay? I'm sorry I brought it up."

Gavin nodded. He scrunched up his face as if squeezing the unhappiness from it. Then he got up and tried to entice a chipmunk to eat some crumbs.

Norah lay down again. Why had she made him so miserable? She watched him crouch patiently until the chipmunk finally snatched a piece of bread from his fingers, and her love for him was so sharp it hurt her inside.

Then Gavin came back and sat beside her. "Norah, there's something very important I want to ask you."

"I thought we weren't going to talk about it any more!" What had she done? Was Gavin going to worry about this from now on?

"It's not *that*. It's about Creature." He pulled the elephant from his pocket.

Norah laughed. She sat up and took Creature from Gavin, sniffing him. "He doesn't smell bad any more— the sun must have baked it out of him. What's the problem? Does he need mending again? I don't think there are any places left to sew!"

"No, he doesn't need mending. It's just that—well, Peter says I'm too old for him," said Gavin. "He makes fun of me for carrying him around."

"But you only do here. In Toronto you leave him in your room when you're at school. And besides, it's none of Peter's business."

"No ... but maybe he's right. It *is* sort of babyish to have a toy elephant when you're eight. Peter and Ross and Sally think I should *bury* him. They want to have a funeral with hymns and a cross, like we do for dead birds. But I *couldn't*!" He grabbed Creature back from Norah and stroked his trunk, close to tears again.

"Bury him! That's absurd. Don't you listen to them, Gavin. Do you still like Creature?"

"Of course," said Gavin in a small voice. "I've had him all my life. But I don't want to be babyish. Maybe I *should* give him up. The way Aunt Bea gave up cigarettes because of her cough."

"You don't have to give him up! Look, I have an idea. Why don't you make Creature your club mascot? Call it the *Elephant* Detective Agency and have an elephant flag and elephant badges. I bet they'd go for that."

"Yes…," said Gavin slowly. "We could tie him to a pole and march around with him. He'd be a sort of—a sort of *joke*. Except to me, of course."

"And no one ever needs to know you feel differently," said Norah. She looked at her watch. "It's time to head back."

As they cleaned up their picnic and walked back to the canoe, she thought about Gavin's strange need for a toy. She'd never understood it. Even as a little girl, she hadn't liked stuffed animals or dolls—she only wanted to *do* things. She and Gavin were so different. But she was glad she'd thought of a way for him to hold on to his best friend.

On the way back they spotted some slate-coloured cranes and a swimming beaver, who slapped his tail as they glided by. Uncle Gerald was waiting at the mouth of the river with the *Florence*. He had George and Denny with him, who squealed with excitement when they saw them.

Before they reached Port Schofield they glimpsed a double-decker steamship with rounded ends and a striped smokestack: the *Sagamo*, returning from her daily Hundred Mile Cruise. As the boat came closer they heard piano music and voices singing "There'll Always Be an England."

"There you go, Norah and Gavin!" grinned Uncle Gerald, as they all waved at the passengers leaning over the railings. "A bit of home for you. Someone told me they sing that when they pass the German prison camp."

Norah sighed. She'd never liked that droning song and she was never going to be allowed to forget that she didn't really belong here. She didn't want to think about England any more. All she wanted to do was to keep "messing about in boats," like Ratty and Mole in *The Wind in the Willows*. To sit here with the lake breeze on her cheeks and the smell of fresh water in her nostrils; to hold on to these precious last weeks of summer—and to Andrew.

15

Lois

O nce again Andrew was spending most of his time with the Mitchells. Norah decided he was probably avoiding the family until he told them his decision. When she pictured him facing the Elders on their last night she sometimes felt frightened for him. But she knew he would be splendid—he would address them regally the way he had when he'd played a prince.

She wondered if Aunt Mary was also going to reveal her secret soon. She hadn't been back to Port Schofield since the wedding and had begun taking long, solitary walks around the island. Perhaps she too was trying to work up her courage until the last evening—then she'd tell them she was going to get married.

For the first time it occurred to Norah that if Aunt Mary got married she wouldn't be living with them. She'd have to move to Regina—wasn't that where she said Tom was from? As much as she wanted Aunt Mary to be happy, it would be awful living with just Aunt Florence. But perhaps Tom would live with them in Toronto. Aunt Florence would probably insist on it, Norah told herself.

How shocked the family was going to be when these two bombshells exploded! Poor Aunt Florence—little did she know that her daughter and her great-nephew were about to make announcements that would shatter her assumptions that all was as it should be.

The cousins were spending every moment soaking up the last few drops of fine weather that the summer was squeezing out. They had several picnics and a late-night bonfire on the shore. Now it was dark by about eight and cool enough to put on sweaters and slacks.

"Brrrr!" shivered Janet one evening, as she and Norah and Clare walked down to the boathouse. "It feels like fall!"

They were escaping from the Elders. A boatload of neighbours had arrived after dinner and the girls had grown tired of sitting politely and responding to the usual inane questions. The worst was, "All ready for school?" One of the visitors was the mother of one of Flo's service-men. She and Flo spent the whole of the evening deep in conversation about Frank. Flo seemed almost like an Elder herself as she took part in the maternal discussion.

"We're going to bed now," Clare announced finally, with a commanding look at Janet and Norah.

"So soon?" asked her mother, but they slipped away before anyone could say more.

"Thanks for getting us out of there," said Janet as they pounded up the boathouse stairs. "What should we do now? It's too cold to go swimming."

Clare looked mysterious and pulled out a thin, rectangular box from under her bed. "I know something we can do." She lit two candles and put them and the box on a low table. They sat cross-legged around it.

"Louise left me this," she explained. "It's called a Ouija board."

"It sounds rude," giggled Janet. "Is it one of those games where you have to tell things about yourself? I'm not playing if it is."

Clare frowned. "It isn't a game—it's real. Do you think you're brave enough to try?"

"Sure!" said Janet, her voice wavering a bit. "Aren't we, Norah?"

Norah shrugged. She wasn't going to let Clare's pose impress her. She eyed the strange board suspiciously as Clare unfolded it. The alphabet was printed in two curving rows in the middle of it, with a line of numbers underneath. YES was in one upper corner and NO in the other. Clare placed a small, heart-shaped wooden platform on top.

"This is the planchette. Two of us have to put our hands on it and ask Ouija a question. Then it moves to the letters or numbers and spells out the answer."

"All by itself?" said Janet, her eyes growing round.

"No, Clare moves it," said Norah. "I've heard of this—it's a trick."

"It is not!" cried Clare. "It really works! Louise and I found out all sorts of things—we know who we're going to marry! *You* don't have to do it, Norah," she added coldly. "Come on, Janet. Put your hands there. That's right, our fingers should just barely touch. Don't put any weight on it. Now—*Ouija, Ouija* …" Her voice sounded ridiculously ghoulish. "Tell us … tell us the name of Janet's future husband."

Janet giggled. "Quiet!" hissed Clare. "You have to concentrate."

They were all silent. The waves lapped softly outside. Then, very slowly, the planchette moved over the board on its three felt-covered feet.

Janet gasped. "Keep your hands on it!" Clare warned her. The tiny table went as far as the letter *H* and stopped.

"That's the first letter of his name," said Clare. "What's next, Ouija?"

Slowly the pointer moved to *A*.

"It's laughing at you," said Norah. "HA!"

The others ignored her. "Now *R*," whispered Janet. "But now it won't move—why not?"

"Is it another *R*?" asked Clare. The planchette swung over to the word yes.

"Har, har," whispered Norah.

"*Y!*" said Clare. "Harry! Is the name 'Harry', Ouija?"

Yes, answered the planchette.

Clare and Janet dropped their hands in their laps. "I told you it worked!" said Clare. "Do you know any Harrys, Janet?"

"No," whispered Janet. Her hands were trembling. "You mean, that's who I'm going to marry?" She began to smile. "That means I'll *get* married one day!"

Norah scowled. "Clare was moving it, Janet. I told you, it's just a trick."

Clare looked disgusted. "All right then—*you* try it, with Janet. Then you can't say I'm moving it. Janet wouldn't cheat."

Norah shrugged and placed her fingers on the planchette.

"Ask it who *you're* going to marry," ordered Clare.

"You ask it," retorted Norah. "I'm not speaking to some dumb board."

"No, it has to be one of you two."

"I'll do it, then," said Janet. "Ouija, Ouija," she crooned, her voice sounding even sillier than Clare's. "Tell us who Norah is going to marry."

Norah waited, confident that the pointer wouldn't move at all. Then it slid across the board so fast she could hardly keep her fingers on it. "Stop it, Janet!" she cried. "I thought you weren't going to cheat!"

"I'm not doing it!" whispered Janet frantically. "Don't let go, Norah!"

"C!" cried Clare triumphantly.

In an instant Norah's mind swept from disbelief to acute disappointment that it wasn't an *A*.

"*A ... N ... T ... S ... A ... Y,*" chanted Clare, as the planchette almost zoomed around, making a tiny scraping sound. "Is that all, Ouija? Yes."

"CANTSAY—what kind of name is that?" said Janet. "Maybe it's a last name."

"No," said Norah suddenly. "It's *can't say*. It doesn't know." That was almost a relief—it still left the possibility open for Andrew.

Then she shivered. It really did seem to work—she knew Janet hadn't been moving it. "Okay," she admitted to Clare. "I believe it now. But I don't believe it's magic. There must be some explanation."

"Louise's father says that we will it to go to certain letters. But *I* think it's supernatural. You can even talk to someone who's dead—do you want to try?"

"No!" shuddered Janet. "That's too spooky. Let's ask it how many children I'm going to have—me and Harry, that is," she snickered.

They crouched around the board again and Norah tried it once more with Janet. A strange thrill washed over her, as if they were doing something forbidden.

"Three!" said Janet. "Good, because that's exactly how many I've always wanted. Ask it how many Clare's going to have."

They couldn't stop now. Again and again they asked questions and the Ouija board obliged them every time. They found out that Clare would have no children and that Norah would have two (so I *will* marry Andrew, she concluded); that Clare would travel and Janet would pass math.

"Ask it when the war will be over," said Norah.

But the Ouija wouldn't budge. "I guess it doesn't know," said Clare. "It can't know everything."

Janet yawned. "I can hardly keep my eyes open."

They heard Flo brushing her teeth below them and hid the Ouija board under Clare's bed again, guessing that she wouldn't approve.

After the others were asleep, Norah tossed restlessly and finally got up again. She shrugged her clothes on over her pyjamas and wandered along the shoreline. Once she was back in the city she was going to miss this freedom of getting up at night if she wanted to.

Two loons called back and forth to each other in a yearning warble. Poring over the Ouija board had made her feel slightly sick, as if she had eaten too much rich food. It had been fascinating and strange, but she didn't want to do it again.

Up in the cottage the lower lights were off and the upper ones on; the Elders must be getting ready for bed. Norah fetched a flashlight from the boathouse and made her way to her rock. She studied the stars and found the Great Bear, which she had now learned to call the Big Dipper. The Northern Lights rippled across the sky in shifting bands of greenish-white. Their majestic, eerie beauty was almost frightening.

Norah glanced down at Andrew's dark cabin. Where was he tonight? If only he were up here, confiding in her again; she began to go over that whole magical encounter, as she had done a million times already.

Just as she began to feel too cold to stay out any longer, she heard the *Putt-Putt* arrive at the dock. Andrew's laugh rang out—someone was with him. A light female voice joined his in singing "Don't Sit Under the Apple Tree." Then two dark figures came into view behind the cottage. In the light from the back windows Norah could make out the other singer—Lois Mitchell.

The two of them hung onto each other and stumbled down the hill to Andrew's cabin. Its windows lit up after they went in. Norah couldn't help slipping down to eavesdrop, even though the longer she heard them together the worse it made her feel.

The window was open a crack. "I can't stay long," Lois was saying.

"Just a little while," said Andrew. "I managed to get two bottles of beer."

"Well ... maybe half an hour," said Lois.

This was just the opposite of the party, when Andrew had been the one to want Lois to go. Now his voice was tender and Norah shook with jealousy. Why am I listening? she asked herself. She was filled with the same kind of self-disgust she'd felt over the Ouija board. But she couldn't seem to leave, and moved farther into the bushes by the window.

"It's so maddening that we're not going to the same university," said Lois. "Will you come and visit me at Queen's?"

Norah was glad to hear the hesitation in Andrew's voice before he mumbled, "I'll have to see." At least he'd only told *her* his secret.

She tried to calm herself. After all, it was normal for Andrew to have girl friends until Norah was old enough to be one. She knew he'd had them before—Janet had told her. And Lois was acting so silly, laughing and teasing—surely he didn't take her seriously.

Andrew and Lois began to dance to their own music,

humming "You'll Never Know." That's *our* song! Norah whispered between clenched teeth. She was relieved to hear them sit down again but now it was worse—the whimpers and endearments of kissing began.

Norah couldn't stand this—she really had to leave. She began to unbend her cramped legs, but Lois's next words made her freeze.

"I'm so lucky that you picked *me,*" she said, in her ironic voice. "Do you realize how many girls are in love with you? Alma Field is crazy about you. So is Ceci Johnson. And that funny little English girl—I saw the way she looked at you that day in town. At the party too— she was watching your every move, and glaring at *me*!"

"Oh, *Norah,*" laughed Andrew. "Yes, she does seem to have a crush on me. I try not to encourage it, but she shadows me like a hawk! She's a good kid, though."

Somehow Norah managed to make her legs move. Forcing her body to be silent, she crept out of the bushes and stumbled up the hill and down the steps to the boathouse, forgetting to use her flashlight. She kicked off her shoes and crawled under the covers without taking her clothes off. Then she crammed her blanket into her mouth so the huge sobs bursting out of her wouldn't wake the others.

A kid. "Oh, *Norah,*" he had said in a dismissing tone. He had *laughed* at her. He had called her love a crush.

He didn't love her. He never had.

A wave of pain crashed over her. "*Ohhh,*" she wailed, hardly caring now if the others woke up. But they slept on. Norah cried until her whole body ached. Then she lay rigid and stared at the wall, not thinking or feeling anything at all.

16

"I'll Never Smile Again"

The next day Andrew and Lois seemed to have become a couple. Andrew invited her for dinner and she came early to spend the afternoon swimming with the family.

"Such a pretty girl," said Aunt Dorothy.

"Very polite, too," added Aunt Bea.

"And she comes from a good family," pronounced Aunt Florence. "I must write to Constance and tell her how much we like her."

The aunts switched to the topic of possible husbands for Princess Elizabeth, as if she, too, were an acquaintance.

"So Lois gets the seal of approval," whispered Flo, lying beside Norah on the dock. "They'll have them married in no time! *I* don't think it's going to last long. She doesn't take him seriously, but he can't see that yet."

Norah glanced at her, surprised to hear Flo sounding jealous too. Maybe it *wouldn't* last. And maybe Lois wouldn't like him any more when she heard that he wasn't going to fight. But even if Andrew stopped seeing Lois, Norah could never forget what he thought of *her*. Andrew was as friendly as ever today but she could only hear "good kid" behind every word he said to her.

The trouble was ... she still loved him. She watched him climb up the ladder, panting and dripping. He shook his wet hair at Lois and his musical laugh rang out when she shrieked.

I don't *want* to love him, thought Norah. But she couldn't help it. The rest of her life was ruined; she would always love him and he would never love her back. All day she kept having to escape from everyone to have a cry—she, who had always been proud of the fact that she *never* cried. She hid her face in her towel as tears threatened once more.

"I'll never smile again," crooned the phonograph they'd brought out onto the dock. Norah dived into the lake to cool her agony.

"Will you be our stage manager, Norah?" Gavin asked her that night. He and the rest of the Fearless Four were putting on a play for the last evening. "We need someone to pull the curtain and things."

"Sure," shrugged Norah. She listened dully while Gavin told her the plot. "Creature is the star!" he grinned.

"I'll help you make some costumes," Norah told him. At least it would give her something to do.

Picking blueberries was another distraction. "With jam about to be rationed I want as many as you can find," Hanny told the children the next morning. Aunt Anne, Aunt Dorothy and Aunt Mary joined Hanny for a jam-making marathon. For a couple of days the sweet heavy scent of cooked berries filled the cottage. Norah helped sterilize jars and melt paraffin. In Toronto she retreated to the kitchen with Hanny whenever Aunt Florence was too much to bear. Now she used this kitchen for a refuge from Andrew.

ON THE AFTERNOON they finished all the berries, Norah sat dully on the dock wondering what to do with herself. *Wuthering Heights* lay abandoned beside her; it was too painful to read a story about love.

The *Putt-Putt* appeared around the point; Andrew's arm waved. Norah jumped up to escape him, but he was calling her name and she had to wait.

"Would you like to go out in the canoe?" he asked as soon as he landed. "There's something I have to talk to you about." Norah flushed—whenever she encountered him she felt ashamed.

"No thanks," she said as coolly as she could manage. She ran up the steps before he could say more.

He tried again that evening, actually turning up at the boathouse when they were getting ready for bed. "Norah!" he called up.

She stuck her head out the window.

"Do you want to go for a walk?"

"No thanks," said Norah. "I'm already in my pyjamas." She withdrew her head quickly, but not before she had seen an apologetic look on Andrew's face. Part of her wondered what he wanted, but she was no longer strong enough to be alone with him, not when she knew what he thought of her.

He probably wants to talk about how he's going to tell the Elders, she decided. Well, he'll just have to work it out by himself. She tried to be angry with him, but she was filled with a rush of yearning. She put out her head again and watched his back as he walked slowly up the steps to the cottage.

"Imagine Norah turning down a walk with Andrew," taunted Clare.

Janet looked puzzled. "But Norah doesn't like Andrew."

"That's right—I don't," said Norah stiffly.

"Then you've changed," said Clare.

"Why did Andrew want to go for a walk with just you?" asked Flo.

Norah shrugged. "How should I know?" She hid under the covers from their curious faces. Why couldn't they just leave her alone? For the first time all summer she looked forward to the privacy of her own room in Toronto.

The next morning Norah was relieved to hear that Andrew had gone to Huntsville for a few days. "Mr. Hancock took him to the train station in Brockhurst," she heard Aunt Dorothy tell Flo. "He won't be back until our last evening. He said he was going to visit some friends of his parents."

NORAH SAT LISTLESSLY at the kitchen table while Aunt Bea and Aunt Mary discussed with Hanny the special menu for their last meal tomorrow.

"It would be lovely to have a roast," said Aunt Bea. "How I miss the supply boats! They came twice a week right to our dock, Norah. There were vegetables and flowers—even a butcher on board! I used to take Gerald down when he was a baby and weigh him on the scales. Now I suppose we'll have to go all the way into Port Clarkson—the best butcher is there."

"I'll go," said Aunt Mary. "If Norah will drive me. Will you?"

"All right," shrugged Norah.

She had never driven the *Putt-Putt* so far and her gloom lifted a bit when Aunt Mary let her manoeuvre the launch through the lock at Port Clarkson all by herself. But she quickly got bored with shopping and followed Aunt Mary around the stores in a dull daze.

"Would you like a cool drink before we go back?" asked her guardian.

"I don't care," said Norah.

They sat in a dim restaurant, sipping iced tea. Aunt Mary's kind face looked concerned. "You've been so pensive the last few days, Norah. Are you worried about going back to school?"

"No," muttered Norah, keeping her eyes down so Aunt Mary wouldn't notice her quick tears. If only she could unload her misery and be comforted! But she didn't want anyone to know how foolish she had been. She looked up, blinking rapidly. "There *is* something, but I can't tell you."

"I won't pry then," said Aunt Mary. "I hope it's not too serious." She sighed. "Perhaps going back to the city will be a good change for all of us. This summer has been so … *intense,* somehow. We need to get back to our regular routines. You'll be glad to see Paige and Bernard again, I imagine."

Norah nodded, puzzled by her words. Surely Aunt Mary wasn't going back to *her* regular routine—wouldn't she announce tomorrow that she would marry Tom?

Aunt Mary pulled out her handkerchief and blew her nose. It was already raw and her eyes were bloodshot. "What a nuisance this hayfever is," she sniffed. "Did you know that people used to come to Muskoka to avoid it? But now I'm sure there's as much ragweed here as there is in the city."

Then the colour slowly rose in Aunt Mary's face. She gave a small cough and looked down. Norah turned around to see who had startled her.

A man had entered the restaurant and was staring at their table, looking as bewildered as Aunt Mary. Then he came over and said softly, "Good-morning, Mary."

"Good-morning, Tom." Norah almost dropped her glass. "This is Norah Stoakes, who's living with us," continued Aunt Mary. "Norah, I'd like you to meet Mr. Montgomery, an old friend of mine."

"How do you do, Mr. Montgomery," said Norah automatically. She gawked at the man as he stood there.

Tom looked even older up close than he had at a distance. His face was seamed with wrinkles and his sparse hair lay in thin white strands across his high forehead. He seemed as shy as Aunt Mary and pushed up his glasses nervously. "Um, shopping, were you?" he asked finally.

"Yes—we're having a big dinner tomorrow and I needed to pick up a roast."

"I borrowed one of the hotel boats to do some shopping myself. May I give you a lift anywhere?"

"No, thank you. We have our own boat. Come along, Norah, we'd better start back before the meat turns." Aunt Mary gathered up parcels and stood up.

"Goodbye then, Tom," she said, holding out her hand.

"Goodbye, Mary," he said gruffly. "Perhaps I'll see you again next summer." He held onto her hand a second, then Aunt Mary turned abruptly and walked out.

Norah hurried after her. What was *that* all about? Was the whole thing off? Aunt Mary sat in the boat facing backwards, so Norah couldn't see her face. But when they reached their own lake she tapped Norah's shoulder. "I don't want to go back to the island just yet. Could you stop in that cove?"

Norah turned the launch into a tiny cove and cut the engine. "Shall I tie it up?" she asked.

"Yes, but we don't need to get out. I just have to collect myself for a few minutes." Then calm, placid Aunt Mary burst into tears.

"Aunt Mary! What's wrong?!" Norah quickly tethered the *Putt-Putt* to an overhanging branch and sat beside her guardian, patting her shoulder awkwardly.

It only lasted a minute or two. Aunt Mary dabbed at her eyes with her handkerchief, blew her nose again, then turned to Norah with a weak smile.

"What a foolish woman I am, Norah! What must you think of me, carrying on like this? I hope I didn't scare you. Perhaps I should explain. You see, I have been ...

keeping company with Mr. Montgomery all month. I've known him for years—he grew up in Toronto—but he was living in the west."

Norah shifted impatiently. Aunt Mary seemed to have forgotten she'd already told her about Tom.

"Then I ran into him at the end of last summer—he'd been spending August at Eden House Resort. We wrote to each other all winter. He sent his letters care of one of my friends—it was the only way I could hide them from Mother. All those times I said I was getting my dress fitted I was also visiting Tom! It was so underhanded and deceitful. I half-expected Mother to catch on, but she didn't. I just couldn't let her know—not until I was absolutely certain of the relationship."

She looked so guilty that Norah cried, "Of course you couldn't!"

Aunt Mary's cheeks grew pink again. "We had such pleasant visits. He really is a remarkably decent man. And then … he asked me to marry him!"

"Oh, Aunt Mary!" Norah wriggled so much that the boat swayed. "That's wonderful! When did he ask you?"

"At Anne's sister's wedding. I knew he'd be there and we managed to slip away during the reception."

"When are you going to tell Aunt Florence?"

Aunt Mary smiled sadly. "I won't have to, Norah, because I said no."

"You said no! But you love him!"

"Probably I do love him. I must say, I came close to saying yes, but I thought about it very carefully. It's too late for me to get married. I'm happy the way I am. I *like* my life in Toronto, with my church and my Red Cross work. I have so many friends there. I don't think I could adjust to living somewhere else. And I'd miss you and Gavin dreadfully! I know you won't be with us forever, but I couldn't be the one to leave first."

"But why can't Tom—Mr. Montgomery, I mean—live with us in Toronto?"

"He could never do that, Norah. He doesn't want to change his life, either. He has relatives in the west— he belongs there now. And there's Mother, of course. I couldn't ask anyone to put up with her and she'll need me more and more as she gets older."

"But that's just like *before*! You didn't get married *last* time because of Aunt Florence! You can't let her ruin your life again!"

"Perhaps, the first time, it was because of Mother," said Aunt Mary. "Not now. If I really wanted to marry him, I wouldn't let her stand in my way. No ... even though she's obviously a factor in my decision, this time it's because of me. I've become used to my own company and my own ways. I don't think I'm prepared to change them, not even for someone I respect as much as I do Tom."

"But ..." Norah's ready tears overflowed. "But you *love* him! And he must love you, if he asked you to marry him. He's your true love, just like all the songs. You have to be loyal to him!"

"Why, Norah! It's not like you to cry! Here, have what's left of my hankie. I shouldn't have told you all this—you're only thirteen, after all. Love seems different when you're young." She smiled. "Despite all those romantic songs, I don't believe that everyone has just one true love—why, look at me!"

"What do you mean?" gulped Norah. "You've only loved Tom! All those years!"

"All those years …" Aunt Mary looked puzzled, then she laughed. "Poor Norah, no wonder you're confused! That was a *different* Tom, that first man I told you about. That's Thomas Young. Now that would be loyalty, if I still loved *him*. I don't even know where he lives now."

"A different Tom?" repeated Norah weakly.

"Yes, it is rather a strange coincidence, isn't it? But after all, it's a common name."

"You mean, now you love someone else?"

"Yes, I do. You *can* love several different people in your life, you know. You will, I'm sure, until you find the right one."

"Never!" cried Norah. "I'll never love anyone but—" She clapped her hand over her mouth and her fingers became slippery with tears.

Aunt Mary picked up the sodden handkerchief and very gently wiped Norah's face. "So that's it," she said softly. "Who is it—Andrew?"

"Yes," whispered Norah. "He doesn't love *me*, though—he never did!"

Aunt Mary pulled her over for a hug. "Oh, Norah, you're so young—very young! This is just the beginning! I'm not going to say you only have a crush. I remember feeling the same way about one of my teachers—love is just as real at any age. But I promise you, you will get over it—and love someone else in time, someone who will love you back. Andrew is very fond of you, I'm sure, but he's so much older, you can't expect him to be interested in you. But wait and see—you're so full of spirit, so pretty. Lots of people are going to love you!"

"But I'm ugly!" burst out Norah. "My nose is too big!

"It's not big at all. Everyone thinks she's ugly at thirteen. *I* did—and when I look at snaps of myself then, I think I looked fine. Besides, it's what *inside* that makes people attractive."

Now she sounded too much like the Sunday School teacher she was. But her kind words warmed Norah. She remembered that pretty, confident girl in the mirror and hope flickered inside her.

"The meat!" said Aunt Mary. "We must be getting back."

"You won't tell anyone about Andrew, will you?" said Norah before she started the engine.

"Of course not! And I know you won't say anything about Tom. They'll both be our own special secrets."

As they drove back to Gairloch, Norah kept her eyes on the waves ahead, pondering the disappointing end of Aunt Mary's romance. She supposed Aunt Mary was doing what she wanted, though.

Her story wasn't going to be so boring. And she couldn't believe that she'd ever love anyone but Andrew.

17

The Last Evening

They arrived back in time to say goodbye to Aunt Catherine. The whole family congregated on the dock to see her off, while the Nugents, who were going to take her to Ottawa, waited in their launch.

When it was Norah's turn to kiss her she wished she could tell Aunt Catherine what Andrew was going to announce when he came back tomorrow. She would be the only member of the family who would be pleased with him. But it was Andrew's secret.

"Goodbye," she said, suddenly shy.

Aunt Catherine kissed her firmly on each cheek. "There! You have a good year, Norah, and I'll see you next summer. In the meantime, don't grow up too fast! There's no hurry, you know—one day you'll be like me and wishing you were young again."

But her spirit seemed as young as ever as she waved vigorously from the departing boat. Norah watched it until it disappeared around the point. She usually forgot about the old woman until she was here again, but somehow, this year, she missed her already.

THE FAMILY was in a flurry as they got ready to leave. Anything that could be nibbled by mice was put into the "tin room" above the stairs. Hanny packed boxes of jam for each family. Neighbours came by in their boats to say goodbye. Everyone was leaving together on Sunday morning, and the precious moments rushed by. Too soon they were all sitting in the dining room for their last Big Dinner.

"Hanny, you've surpassed yourself." Uncle Reg leaned back in his chair and patted his stomach. "That was the best meal we've had all summer."

"Thank you, sir," said Hanny. She removed his dessert plate, stained purple from blueberry pie. The adults lingered at the table, smoking and chatting.

"The last time we'll all be together," sighed Aunt Bea.

"All except Andrew," sniffed Aunt Florence. "Why couldn't he have gone to Huntsville earlier in the month? And he really should have tried to be back in time for our last dinner. How is he getting here from Brockhurst?"

"He asked Mr. Hancock to leave the *Putt-Putt* there for him," said Uncle Gerald. "He towed it over this afternoon."

"He did promise he'd be back as soon as he could, Aunt Florence," said Aunt Dorothy. She tried to change the subject. "I hope our tires will hold out long enough to come up next year. But I suppose we could take the train."

"It's the gas coupons I'm worried about," said Uncle Barclay. "We may have to run just one boat next summer."

"Why don't you do what we're going to?" said Aunt Florence. "Store the car all year and take streetcars. Then we can save our gas coupons for the trip north and use the rest for the boats."

"Do you want to have another contest, Florence?" asked Uncle Reg. "The first person to make *two* cushion covers by Christmas contributes fewer coupons." He smiled smugly; he'd beaten Aunt Florence by six rows.

"Oh, *you* ... you're just like an old woman," chuckled Aunt Florence. "All right, you're on."

Uncle Barclay began explaining to them once more all the details of the Allied invasion of Italy. Ever since they'd heard the news yesterday he'd talked of nothing else. Finally Gavin got up and whispered to Aunt Florence.

She stood. "All right, everyone, into the living room! I believe we're about to be entertained."

A few minutes later Norah stood behind a sheet pinned over a rope that was stretched across the alcove in the living room. Behind her the Fearless Four whispered last-minute instructions to each other. Norah remembered the unbearable excitement before the curtain rose. Janet, Bob, Alec and she also used to put on plays for the family. But last summer, suddenly feeling self conscious, they'd stopped.

"*Now,* Norah!" hissed Sally. Norah drew back the sheet in jerky movements, careful to keep herself concealed behind it. Then she slipped out at the side to watch the play.

Gavin stood in front of the audience dressed in Uncle Reg's tweed hat, Flo's trench coat pulled up over its belt and Uncle Barclay's pipe in his mouth. "The Fearless Four Detective Agency presents ... The Case of the Stolen Elephant!"

The long play—Gavin had told Norah they couldn't agree on whose ideas to use, so they'd kept in everyone's— was complicated and far-reaching, with many costume changes and allusions to Johnny Canuck, Mussolini, Toad and Sherlock Holmes. They made up a lot of it as they went along, hauling up members of the audience to give evidence. Creature, of course, was the stolen elephant. He was finally given back in the end, returned by Roy Rogers—Peter, resplendent in a cowboy hat and holsters. Then the cast burst into song. "*Off* he goes, into the *wild blue yonder* ..." they shouted, hurling Creature up to the ceiling again and again. He lost his remaining ear on his final landing.

By the time they took their final bows the audience was almost on the floor with laughter. They applauded wildly, wiping tears from their eyes.

"That was *superb*!" said Aunt Florence. "I haven't seen anything like it since Andrew and Flo performed *Dracula* for us. Come and give me a kiss, Gavin."

"Where *is* Andrew?" asked Clare. "Shouldn't he be back by now?"

"I can't think what's keeping him," said Aunt Bea, looking worried.

"Oh, he's probably having too good a time," said Uncle Reg. "You women coddle him too much. Now for some songs!" He pulled out the piano bench and they all gathered round.

For an hour they sang the family favourites: "You Are My Sunshine," "Waltzing Matilda" and "The Quartermaster's Store." All the Drummonds had strong voices. Norah let hers blend in with theirs, glad to forget herself and just sing. Squeezed in between Janet and Aunt Mary, she felt for a while as mindlessly content as she'd been in other summers.

"Here's one for you and Gavin, Norah," said Uncle Reg. He picked out a slow, sentimental melody as they all crooned "There'll be bluebirds over the white cliffs of Dover." Tears gleamed in Aunt Mary's eyes at the words "And Jimmy will go to sleep / In his own little room again." When Uncle Reg stopped playing everyone was looking at Norah and Gavin in the soppy way they sometimes did, when they remembered how far away from home the two of them were.

"I don't think there *are* bluebirds in England," said Norah, trying to change their mood.

"Maybe next summer the war will be over and you won't be here any more!" said Janet suddenly.

"Next summer?" whispered Gavin.

Aunt Florence frowned at Janet and pressed Gavin to her side. "Let's just take things one day at a time. Play something rousing, Reg. How about 'Roll Out the Barrel'?"

"... and the GANG'S—ALL—HERE!" they finished raucously. Everyone collapsed into chairs, while Aunt Mar and Aunt Dorothy handed around coffee.

Uncle Reg was staring intently at Gavin and Bosley. The dog's silky head rested on Gavin's knee; he stroked it sadly.

"I have a proposition for you, Gavin."

"What, Uncle Reg?"

"How would you like to take care of Bosley for me until the end of the war? I'll lend him to you! After all, he's much more attached to you than to me—aren't you, you fickle beast?" Bosley thumped his tail politely, then pressed his head harder against Gavin.

"Give Bosley to *me*?" the little boy breathed.

"*Lend* him. You'll have to give him back when you leave Canada."

"But won't you miss him?"

"Of course I will, but I think Bosley has shown whom he likes the best. I can see him in the holidays."

"Reg Drummond!" Aunt Florence glared at her brother. "Don't you see how cruel your suggestion is? *I've* sometimes thought of getting Gavin a pet, but then he'd have to go through the misery of giving it up. It's out of the question."

"Oh, *please,* Aunt Florence," begged Gavin. "I understand. I know it's just borrowing, really I do."

Aunt Florence looked at his pleading face and sighed. "Oh all right, sweetness. Reg hasn't left me any choice, announcing it this way. But you'll have to walk and feed him every day."

"I will!" promised Gavin. "Thank you, Aunt Florence and Uncle Reg! Did you hear that, Norah? Bosley's coming to live with us! *Aren't* you, Boz …" He buried his head in the dog's neck.

Norah agreed with Aunt Florence. Uncle Reg had set up a situation that was going to be wrenching sometime in the future. But Gavin's pleasure right now was too acute to deny. And it *would* be fun to have a dog in the house, especially a dog as agreeable as Bosley.

Janet and Clare had just started picking teams for Charades when a boat engine sounded faintly.

"Andrew, at last!" said Aunt Florence.

The family waited quietly while they listened to his footsteps on the verandah. Norah wondered why they thudded so heavily—almost like marching. The screen door clacked behind him and then Andrew made his entrance.

Aunt Bea shrieked. Then there was a stunned silence until everyone began to cry out at the same time. "Andrew! Oh, Andrew, my dear boy!"

Norah's arms and legs turned to mush. She shivered violently as she stared at him, her mouth twitching and tears escaping as she realized what he'd done.

Andrew was in uniform—encased from head to feet in thick wool khaki, his trousers billowing over heavy black boots. Worst of all, his beautiful wavy hair had been cropped close to his head, making him look tough and raw, as if all his former grace had been chopped away.

"I'm sorry to give you such a fright," he said quietly, sitting down beside Aunt Florence. "It was the only way I could think of to tell you. I've joined up. Tomorrow afternoon I report to training camp."

"But *why*?" cried Flo. "I thought you were going to wait until you could go over as an officer!"

"*I* know why—you're afraid of missing it, aren't you?" said Uncle Barclay. He clapped Andrew on the shoulder.

"Good for you, boy. I don't blame you—I was hoping you'd do this."

Aunt Florence was finally able to speak. "You've given us all a dreadful shock, Andrew," she said sternly. "You could have at least consulted with us. Or your parents. Do they know?"

"Not yet," admitted Andrew. "I'll phone them tomorrow. Mother will be upset, but she'll come around."

Aunt Florence sniffed. "I should think she would be upset! Her only son, going off to war as a private!" Then she sighed. "I have to admit, I can't blame you either, Andrew. I was hoping—we all were—that you'd be an officer before you went. But Barclay is right—there might not be time for that. I think you've made a very courageous decision."

Then they all swarmed around him. The women were tearful and the men asked questions about training camp. Sally climbed on his lap and played with the tabs on his belt. Ross put on his cap and the other little boys gazed at him with awe.

Norah managed to slip out of the room before anyone noticed how hard she was crying. She ran up to her rock and threw herself down on it, her scalding tears running into the lichen.

How *could* he? He had broken his promise! He had betrayed her, but worse than that, he had betrayed himself—for she couldn't believe he had changed his beliefs so suddenly.

Lois must have talked him into it. She must have wanted him to be a hero—as Norah once had—and persuaded him to join the war like her brother Jack. That was the only explanation that made any sense.

She couldn't get out of her head the shock of seeing him standing there like a stranger. An anonymous soldier, who would crouch in a ditch and shoot people, like the scenes in newsreels.

Another picture flashed into Norah's mind, one she had also seen at the movies again and again. Soldiers lying inert on the ground. *Dead.*

"Doesn't it seem intolerable and absurd to you that whenever human beings disagree they go out and *kill* each other?" Andrew's words, spoken with so much conviction on this rock a short time ago, seemed to ring out again.

Norah thought of the picture of Hugh—Hugh in a uniform as well, gazing at the camera so cheerfully. He had never come back to Gairloch.

Andrew could be killed. His honest eyes, that had looked so enormous in his shorn head, could lose their sparkle forever. Norah had never seen a dead person, but she thought of the glazed eyes of lifeless birds.

War *was* wrong! She didn't care what the cause was. Aunt Catherine was right. It was wrong and wicked that the lives of boys like Andrew and Hugh could be extinguished as easily as snuffing out a candle. When she imagined Andrew lying dead in a muddy ditch somewhere, she knew that she had never really loved him until now.

Norah sat, shivering, drained and bitter, staring at the lake. All she wore was a cotton dress and her bare arms and legs were freezing; but she couldn't move.

"Norah?"

Andrew's voice was hesitant. "I knew I'd find you here." He climbed up beside her. She swivelled to keep her back to him.

"Look, let me explain! I tried to before, but you wouldn't let me."

"I don't want to hear," spat Norah. "Go away!"

"I'm sorry, but you *have* to hear. I know I broke my promise. But I think I have good reason to. And I thought you'd be pleased! After all, now I'm going to fight Hitler—and everything he represents. That's what you wanted me to do, isn't it?"

She whirled around. "Not any more! Now I think it's terrible that you're going to fight! I can't believe you've changed so much. How could you? Was it Lois? Did *she* make you?"

"It has nothing to do with Lois. She knows—I told her before I went to Huntsville—but she didn't affect my decision. It was Jack. I had an incredible letter from him. He *hates* the war—you're too young to hear some of the terrible things he described. Now he hates it as much as I do. But the point is, Norah—he's *still fighting*. He's still over there, doing all the dirty work—he and all the other poor guys—while I sit here smugly saying I won't go. It's not *fair* that they're all suffering—and believe me, they are—while I'm not. I don't want to do it one bit more than I did before but it has to be done. So I may as well do it *now*."

"But you'll have to *kill* people!" cried Norah. "How are you going to do that, after all you said before?"

The muscle in Andrew's cheek jumped violently. "I can't answer that, Norah. All I can say is that—maybe—the end result will be worth it. Don't you see?"

"No, I *don't* see! What if everyone in the world just refused to fight? Then there wouldn't *be* any war! Then no one would get killed! Then y-you wouldn't ..." she choked, starting to sob again.

Andrew pulled her close to him. "You're right. But we don't live in a world like that—not yet, anyway. But maybe if we win this war we'll never have to have another one."

"Aunt Catherine said people felt like that about the *first* world war!"

Andrew gave a weary sigh. "I guess they did ... Norah, I've run out of arguments. All I know is, I've made up my mind. I don't *want* to do it. It's kind of like acting. I'll pretend to do it."

"But—" Then she looked up at his face and saw how determined it was. He wore a new firmness, as unyielding as his uniform. That was why he hadn't been able to tell them until he was wearing it, she realized; the uniform was part of the acting, like a costume. Surely the real Andrew was still underneath.

There was nothing more she could say. She continued to cry quietly, enclosed in the sheltering circle of Andrew's arm. At last she wiped her eyes with the rough wool of his sleeve.

"I'll never, *ever* agree with you," she muttered.

"I don't expect you to," said Andrew. "You're certainly unpredictable, though!" he added.

"So are you!" They exchanged wary smiles.

"Can I write to you?" whispered Norah.

"Of course you can! And you'll still be seeing me every now and then. I'll get leaves until we go over and I'll come and visit you all in Toronto."

Norah stood up and rubbed her goose-pimpled arms. Andrew stood too and they gazed out at the full moon streaming across the peaceful lake. "Whenever I see the moon I'll think of Gairloch," he said softly.

Whenever I see it, I'll think of *you,* thought Norah.

She took a deep breath. *Say* it. Quickly, while she still had him alone.

"Andrew, I—I ..."

He bent over, put his hands on her shoulders and kissed the top of her head. "I know, Norah. I know. And I feel very flattered—I don't think I deserve it. But you're only—I hate to hurt your feelings but—"

Norah sighed. "I'm only thirteen."

"Well ... yes! But the nicest thirteen-year-old I know." He looked apologetic. "I'm really beat, Norah. Are you okay now? Do you mind if I go to bed?"

"I'm okay."

He squeezed her hand, then slipped down the rock towards his cabin.

Norah watched him go, pressing the hand he had touched to her mouth. She stayed on the rock for a long time, the moon a watery blur through her tears.

18

"You'll Never Know"

Everything was packed. The piano had been pushed into its mouse-proof case and the water had been turned off. Already the launches had made several trips to Ford's Bay with suitcases and boxes. Now all the boats had been hoisted to the rafters of the boathouse. Most of the family was gathered on the dock and the verandah, waiting for Mr. McGuigan from the store to appear with his boat and start taking them in batches over to the mainland.

Uncle Gerald and Andrew were fastening the heavy shutters back on the windows. Norah always hated this part about leaving. It was as if the cottage were having its eyes covered.

"School the day after tomorrow!" gloated Clare. "I can hardly wait to see John."

"Oh, Norah, I'll miss you!" wailed Janet. "Christmas seems so far away."

"I think you should all have Christmas with *us* this year," smiled Aunt Dorothy. "Would you like that, Norah? You could come on the train. After all, you should see Montreal before you leave Canada."

"That would be fun," said Norah. She grinned at Janet. "You can play me all your new Frankie records."

"Next summer I'll take you all on a canoe trip to Algonquin Park," said Flo. "If I'm not in the RCAF by then," she added, avoiding her mother's look.

"*Nor*-ah … Aunt Florence says it's our turn first," called Gavin from the dock.

After an almost sleepless night, Norah had risen at dawn, circled the island and said her customary goodbye to every rock and tree. She had kissed all the Elders and now she hugged Janet and Flo.

"What about *me*?" demanded Clare. They stared at each other, then each managed a tight smile.

Then Norah looked around to say goodbye to Andrew. She found him at the far end of the verandah, putting up the last shutter. His ugly uniform still made her quake. In the daylight she noticed the white strip of skin around his haircut where his tan stopped.

Andrew turned around. Norah's heart thumped so loudly she was sure he could hear it. She had rehearsed her last words all night but all she could manage was, "Goodbye, Andrew."

He took her hand, smiling ruefully. "Goodbye, Norah. I'll see you in Toronto." She sped down to the dock.

Gairloch receded into the distance. Aunt Mary sat in the stern of the boat and looked sadly back at the island. Gavin clutched Bosley. Norah's eyes were fixed on the tall boy who stood on the verandah of the cottage and waved after them, looking smaller and more fragile every second.

"Do you think we *will* be back next summer?" Gavin whispered to her after they had landed at Ford's Bay.

"I'm sure we will," said Norah, as much to reassure herself as him. "Don't worry about it any more, Gavin. Let's just enjoy being in Canada. Think of school—you'll be glad to see your friends, won't you?"

"Sure! And wait until they meet Boz! Will you like seeing *your* friends?"

Norah nodded. She crouched by the shore and dabbled her hands in the lake one last time, while the others walked towards the car. She wondered how Paige's summer in Cape Cod had been, and if Bernard and his mother had been able to get away from the hot city. Then she pictured describing *her* summer to them. There was so much of it she'd never be able to explain.

What would the next years bring? Andrew would go off to the war … and *surely*, she prayed, return. She and Gavin would go back to England. Now that she had someone new to worry about, the future seemed more scary and uncertain than ever.

But one thing wasn't uncertain. She would always love him, she told herself fiercely. It was just like her favourite song; he would never know how much. Whatever the future brought, all she could do was hold on to the hope that, one day, he would know—and love her back.

I'm only thirteen, thought Norah. I can wait.

"Norah Stoakes!" called Aunt Florence's exasperated voice. "Are you going to stand there daydreaming all day?"

Norah ran to the car and climbed in. "Sorry," she said cheerfully. "Aunt Florence ... when we get back to Toronto, could you buy me a pair of saddle shoes?"

ACKNOWLEDGEMENTS

For their encouragement, advice, memories and cottages, many thanks to: Sue Alderson; Miza Jean-marie; Mary and George Johnson; Carol, Paul, Mollie and Connie Johnson; Vicki, Stuart, Sanders—and Bosley!—Lazier; Claire Mackay; Hugh, Anne and Matthew Mackenzie; Lee, Mike and Megan Mackenzie; Kay and Sandy Pearson; Linda Shineton and Gordon Mitchell; Hope Thomson, and Calla and Josie Haynes; and Maggie Wedd.

PERMISSIONS

THE LONG AWAITED NEW NOVEL BY KIT PEARSON IS NOW AVAILABLE!

A Perfect Gentle Knight tells the story of the six Bell children, each of them coping in different ways in the aftermath of their mother's death. Seen through the eyes of eleven-year-old Corrie, the story illustrates how a rich fantasy life can sometimes get in the way of reality. While elder sister Roz is growing up and out of the desire for fantasy games, eldest brother Sebastian, who fancies himself Sir Lancelot in their Round Table Game, continues to need them as much as ever, creating tension in the family. Corrie becomes concerned and worries that Sebastian may have lost his grip on what's real.

"Pearson's books are a window to another age.... Pearson has shown her ability ... with grace, sensitivity and a good grasp of what moves and motivates children in any era."—*Toronto Star*

www.kitpearson.ca

ALSO IN THE
GUESTS OF WAR TRILOGY!

WINNER OF THE MR. CHRISTIE BOOK AWARD, THE GEOFFREY BILSON AWARD FOR HISTORICAL FICTION FOR YOUNG PEOPLE, AND THE CANADIAN LIBRARY ASSOCIATION'S BOOK OF THE YEAR FOR CHILDREN

It is the summer of 1940, and all of England fears an invasion by Hitler's army. Still, ten-year-old Norah Stoakes is shocked when her parents decide to send her and her younger brother, Gavin, to Canada as war guests. Travelling across the ocean is an adventure, but Norah's new life in Canada is a bigger challenge that she ever expected. Until, that is, Norah discovers a surprising responsibility that helps her accept her new country and her new home.

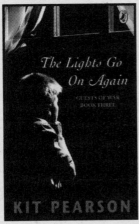

WINNER OF THE IODE VIOLET DOWNEY AWARD AND THE GEOFFREY BILSON AWARD FOR HISTORICAL FICTION FOR YOUNG PEOPLE

It has been five years since Norah and Gavin arrived in Canada, and how that the war is ending, they will soon be going back to England. Norah is eager to see her parents again, but ten-year-old Gavin barely remembers them. He doesn't want to leave his Canadian family, his two best friends, and his dog. Then something happens that forces Gavin to make the most difficult decision of his life.

"A first rate trilogy..."
—The Globe and Mail

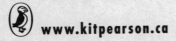

www.kitpearson.ca